GERALD VERNER

THE TOKEN

Complete and Unabridged

LINFORD
Leicester

First published in Great Britain

First Linford Edition
published 2019

A catalogue record for this book is available
from the British Library.

ISBN 978–1–4448–4018–6

Published by
F. A. Thorpe (Publishing)
Anstey, Leicestershire

Set by Words & Graphics Ltd.
Anstey, Leicestershire
Printed and bound in Great Britain by
T. J. International Ltd., Padstow, Cornwall

This book is printed on acid-free paper

1

The Coming of the Bells

The great Julian Shuberg was in a vile temper. There was nothing unusual in this, as the unhappy victims who came under his directorial sway at the Corinthian Film Corporation could have testified, for they were used to his outbursts. Mostly, however, they suffered in silence, since even his worst enemy had to admit that he was one of the best directors who ever bullied a leading lady into hysterics.

On this bright spring morning, however, he was even worse than usual, and nobody could say that he had not just and sufficient cause for being annoyed.

The final scenes of his latest epic, *Lover Come Back*, featuring Gloria Swayne and Richard Sinclair, two of the most popular stars who had ever appeared on the screen, were being shot. The set was ready, groups of alert men waited for the signal to switch on the powerful sun-arcs, the cameraman had got his machine into position, the sound apparatus had been tested, and everything was just as it should be — except Richard Sinclair. He had strolled off the set at five to ten, remarking to Gloria that he would only be a moment, and had not returned.

'Where the devil can that fellow have gone to?' shouted Mr. Shuberg, his fat face red with anger. 'This is an outrage! An unheard-of thing!' He ran his hands through his thick grey hair, almost dancing in his excitement. 'Go and find the man!' he screamed, turning to his assistant who was standing by. 'Find him and bring him here at once! I will *not* have my work ruined by Sinclair, star or no star!'

The man hurried away, and Mr. Shuberg made an impatient gesture towards the rest of the cast. 'You can take it easy,' he grunted. 'We can't do anything until that fellow is found. What the devil does he think he's playing at? Does he think we've got all the time in the world? Some of these people make me sick!

They're more trouble than they're worth!'

The Corinthian Film Corporation worked to a schedule, and Mr. Shuberg had to account to an unsympathetic board of directors for every minute that a film took to complete after its allotted time. The final scenes of this particular picture had already proved difficult. The preceding two days had been spent in rehearsing — rehearsing until everyone had grown sick and tired of going over the same monotonous action. Everyone, that was, with the exception of Mr. Shuberg himself, who never seemed to tire, but would spend hours over the tiniest detail until it came up to his critical standard. 'We shan't get the thing finished today at this rate!' he grumbled to Gloria Swayne. 'Where did he go to? What did he want to leave for?'

She remained tactfully silent. She had had experience of Mr. Shuberg in these moods, and it had taught her that silence was the best policy.

'He knew we were going right ahead,' went on the director. 'What the deuce he wanted — '

The remainder of his sentence was drowned in a shrill scream that came echoing through the studio, and swinging round in the direction of the unexpected sound, he saw a white-faced woman come stumbling towards him.

'What's the matter with *you*, Miss Banks?' he snapped. 'Seen a mouse or something?'

'Mr. Shuberg — Oh, Mr. Shuberg,' the continuity woman spoke huskily and with difficulty, 'over there! Behind that screen. Oh my God, it was dreadful — '

'What was dreadful? What the hell are you talking about?' Shuberg stared at her frightened face balefully, but she could only stab jerkily with a shaking finger towards a dark comer of the studio.

With a muttered oath, the incensed director strode over to the place she indicated and peered at the pile of furniture and oddments that had been cleared from a previous set and stacked there in readiness for removal to the property room.

At first he could see nothing to explain Miss Banks's terror; and then, as he was angrily turning away, he caught sight of a patent leather shoe that projected from behind a Chinese screen.

With a startled exclamation, he pulled the screen aside and stared down at that which it had concealed. He would have to wait a long time for Richard Sinclair to finish his love scene! The film star lay upon his back amid a litter of studio rubbish, his immaculate shirt front red and wet, and it needed no expert eye to see that he was dead!

Mr. Shuberg, his anger dispelled, gazed at the ivory hilt of the knife that protruded from the centre of the crimson welter, and his expression was that of a man who felt suddenly sick.

The red was gone from his flabby face when he turned away and walked unsteadily back to the group by the camera.

'What is it?' asked Gloria Swayne anxiously, touching his arm. 'What's happened?'

'Something rather dreadful, my dear,' answered the director a little shakily, and pulling out a silk handkerchief, mopped away the beads of perspiration that had gathered on his forehead. 'It's Sinclair;

he's — he's dead . . . It looks like murder . . . '

'Murder!' She breathed the word almost inaudibly, and her blue eyes widened. 'Murder — Dick? But it's impossible . . . He hadn't an enemy in the world . . . Nobody would want to kill him . . . '

'I'm afraid somebody has,' said Shuberg, recovering from his first shock. 'Tom!' he called harshly to a youthful-looking man who, in spite of his boyish appearance, was approaching forty. 'Dismiss everybody and then phone the police. There'll be no more work done today.' And then as a thought struck him he added quickly: 'No, wait a minute. Don't send anyone away yet. Keep everybody in the building until the police arrive. My God, this is terrible!'

He wiped his face again and sank into the chair which was reserved for his use.

Gloria, her face haggard and drawn, stared fearfully towards the shadowy place where the dead man lay. 'It can't be true,' she murmured huskily. 'It can't be true . . . '

6

Mr. Shuberg reached up and patted her arm sympathetically. 'I'm afraid it is, my dear,' he said gently. 'You'd better go to your dressing-room. It's bad enough for all of us, but it's worse for you.' He looked round and beckoned to a frightened dresser. 'Take Miss Swayne to her room,' he ordered; and with a dazed look in her big eyes, she allowed herself to be taken away.

The woman who had made the discovery was sobbing quietly on a big settee that formed part of the furniture for the set. Rising to his feet, Mr. Shuberg walked over to her and laid his hand on her shoulder. She started up with a little cry at his touch.

'Now, now, Carrie,' he said soothingly, 'it's only me. Pull yourself together. You'd better go along to the canteen and get a stiff brandy and soda.'

With his assistance, she got to her feet. 'Was it — how — ' she began incoherently, but he checked her with a gesture.

'Don't talk about it and don't think about it,' he said. 'You'll have enough thinking and talking to do presently.'

When she had gone, he went back to his chair by the camera and sat, staring gloomily in front of him. He was still sitting thus when the police arrived.

A thick-set florid-faced man detached himself from the group who came into the studio and approached him. 'Got your message, sir,' he said gruffly. 'My name is Shadgold. I'm a detective-inspector of the C.I.D., and I happened to be in the station when your phone call came through. Something pretty serious has happened here, I understand?'

Mr. Shuberg briefly explained, and Shadgold pursed his thick lips.

'Hm!' he said noncommittally. 'Where's the body?'

'Over there — behind that screen,' answered Shuberg, pointing. 'Nothing has been touched, Inspector, and nobody has left the building, with the exception of one of my assistants who went over to the office to telephone.'

'Thank you, sir,' said Shadgold, and he turned to the group of men who had accompanied him. 'Come along, we'd better get busy.'

They moved over to the corner where the body lay, followed uneasily by Mr. Shuberg, and watched by the rest of the people in the big studio. After a cursory glance at the dead man, Shadgold nodded to the police doctor who had come with him, and he made a hurried examination.

'The man died instantly,' he reported when this had been completed. 'He was killed with an upward stab that passed through the heart, and the murderer made no attempt to pull the knife out. I shouldn't think this poor fellow knew what had happened to him. There'll have to be an autopsy, of course.'

Shadgold grunted and rubbed his chin. 'I suppose you've no idea who was responsible for this man's death, sir?' he asked, turning to Shuberg, and the director shook his head.

'No idea at all, Inspector!' he declared. 'The whole thing's a mystery to me.'

The Scotland Yard man frowned, still staring at the sprawling figure of the dead star. 'Hm!' he remarked at last. 'Your photographers had better do their stuff, Martin.'

The local inspector, who had come with him, nodded and issued a string of orders to his men. 'Now we can move him,' said Shadgold when the usual police photographs had been taken. 'Pick him up and carry him over to that settee there.'

Two uniformed men gently raised the body and laid it on the big couch. The good-looking face of the actor was serene even in death. Save for the unnatural pallor and the grim stain that marred the whiteness of his evening shirt front, he might have been in a deep sleep.

Shadgold looked down at him thoughtfully, his heavy face expressionless. 'Now, Mr. Shuberg,' he began, 'I should like — ' He broke off, stooped, and peered more intently at the recumbent form. 'What the devil is that?' he muttered.

'What?' asked Inspector Martin eagerly.

Shadgold pointed, and following the direction of his stubby finger, Martin saw what it was that had attracted his attention, and his brows drew together.

The wide lapel of the dead man's dress coat had fallen away; and pinned on the underside, just beneath the button-hole, was a small object that glittered in the light of the pilot lamps. It was a tiny bell, a tawdry thing of silvered metal, and Shadgold stared at it in wonder.

During the weeks that followed, he was to see many such tokens and in similar circumstances. For the menace of the silver bells that had come to the studio of the Corinthian Film Corporation on that bright spring morning was destined to spread far and wide over the land, bringing death and terror in its wake.

2

The Terror Spreads

Inspector Martin was the first to find his voice. 'Funny thing for a man to carry around,' he remarked. 'Mr. Shuberg!'

'What is it?' enquired the stout director, coming reluctantly forward.

'Have you seen this thing before, sir?' The inspector pointed to the little token. 'Was it a lucky charm or something of that sort? I've heard that these people go in for that sort of thing.'

Shuberg looked at the tiny object, frowned, and shook his head. 'No, I haven't,' he declared. 'I don't think Sinclair was a superstitious man. Perhaps Miss Swayne could tell you. She's worked with him a great deal.'

Gloria was sent for and came immediately. In the interval, she had removed her film make-up, and her face was pale and she looked ill.

'No, I've never seen Dick with anything

12

like that,' she answered huskily when the question was put to her. 'I know show people are superstitious and carry all sorts of charms, but Dick was rather sceptical of anything of the sort.' Her voice shook a little, and it was obvious she was only keeping control of her emotions by an effort.

'Maybe it's nothing,' grunted Shadgold, frowning. 'Thank you, Miss Swayne. We're sorry to have troubled you.'

At his signal, Shuberg took her arm and led her gently away.

'You'd better take statements from everybody in here, Martin,' went on the inspector. 'I'll question the outside staff and see if they can throw any light on the crime. We're going to have a difficult job.'

His words were prophetic. Just how difficult he was going to find it he didn't realise, for despite all his efforts and the most exhaustive enquiries on the part of the local police, nothing came to light to give them the slightest clue, either to the perpetrator of, or the motive for, the murder. More than once during the days that followed, Shadgold wished fervently that he could consult his friend Trevor Lowe; but since the dramatist was at that moment recuperating in a little Spanish village after three months of strenuous work, the wish was futile.

Inquiries revealed the fact that Richard Sinclair had had, apparently, no enemies. Nor did there seem any reason why his life should have been cut short in such a ruthless manner. For so popular a figure, he had lived simply; and apart from his work, he did not appear to have had any interests that could have supplied or suggested a motive for his death.

One ingenious theory put forward by some irresponsible person was that a rival film company had hired an assassin to kill Sinclair in order to hold up the completion of the film; but this far-fetched suggestion was discounted immediately.

As Shadgold had predicted, it was not an easy matter to check up on the number of potential murderers who might have been at the studio that morning. The employees of the corporation numbered some hundreds, and there had been three studios at work, which necessitated a large number of extras as well as the usual staff. The number amounted, altogether, to some four hundred and fifty people, any one of whom could have been responsible for the killing.

It was discovered that the murder weapon belonged to the studio. It was a heavy throwing knife with an ivory handle, and could easily have been picked up by any unauthorised person. The hilt was subjected to the usual tests, but was found to be devoid of fingerprints of any kind.

Gradually public interest in the case waned, and it disappeared from the front pages of the newspapers, being relegated to small paragraphs elsewhere; and the killing of Richard Sinclair was almost forgotten, except by the men who still worked patiently at Scotland Yard sifting the meagre information at their disposal and trying to acquire more.

And then occurred a fresh sensation which once again brought it prominently before the public.

Three weeks after the murder, a carter was driving his horse homewards to the small village of Midthorpe in Sussex. His way led through a shaded part of the road, and he was urging the animal forward when it suddenly shied at something. Stopping to see what it was, the carter was horrified to discover the body of a well-dressed middle-aged man lying in the road with a gunshot wound in his head. When the police arrived from the neighbouring town of Horsham, it was discovered that the body was that of George Stone, a retired grocer, who lived at Grey Gables, a large detached house a mile or two out of the town.

At first sight, there was nothing to connect the two crimes, until an intelligent local inspector discovered the small silver bell that had been pinned to the underside of the lapel of the dead man's coat.

The newspapers seized eagerly on the bizarre aspect of the two crimes. 'The Bell Murders', as they were called, occupied the greater part of the front pages, and public excitement grew to fever heat when a week after the discovery of Stone's body Solomon Riess, a well-known diamond merchant of Hatton Garden, was found hanging in the grounds of his house at Golder's Green with one of the bells attached to his coat. The police had barely completed the preliminary examinations in connection with this third crime when a fourth occurred.

A young journalist living at Hendon telephoned to the *Daily Sun* the information that the body of a local undertaker had been found in his shop. His head had been battered in with a heavy piece of marble, and fastened to his coat was the now familiar token.

This was the fourth murder committed within the space of just over a month, and each crime, although seemingly unconnected, was nevertheless allied by the same sinister little emblem.

Scotland Yard was quite frankly at its wits' end to find any person on whom the guilt could be pinned. The retired grocer had led the most blameless of lives; and although Solomon Riess had not been without his business enemies, these had come forward at the request of the police and accounted satisfactorily for their movements at the time when he must have met his death. As for the undertaker, this seemed the most senseless and wanton killing of the four.

The general theory was that a maniac was at large; there seemed no other way to account for the apparent haphazard selection of the victims. A homicidal lunatic whose mania prompted him to decorate the people he killed with the fantastic little token.

The prominence given by the newspapers to the crimes caused the general public to become alarmed. People spoke in hushed voices of the advent of a second Jack the Ripper, and something like a panic spread over the country; for none knew when or where the hand of the unknown killer would strike next.

Among the many millions of people in England were literally hundreds who walked in terror; yet those who had most reason to fear were unaware of the danger in which they lived, or how near the menace of the silver bells was to them.

3

Trevor Lowe Is Interested

Mr. Trevor Lowe, that eminent dramatist, arrived back in London on a grey morning when the streets were wet and shining and a drizzle of rain was falling incessantly. The contrast between this unpleasant weather and the sunshine of Spain was depressing; but he was glad, all the same, to be back.

Although he had enjoyed his holiday, the weeks of enforced idleness had begun to irk him. He was never happier than when working at high pressure, and it had only been after the peremptory orders of his doctor that he had gone at all. Months of strenuous mental work, however, had been succeeded by what was tantamount to a nervous breakdown, and the specialist had been insistent.

'If you don't go away for a month, Lowe,' he declared decisively, 'I wash my hands of the consequences! It's better to take a month off than be incapacitated for a year.'

The force of this argument was so apparent that the dramatist reluctantly agreed. He had completed all his important work, and leaving his secretary, Arnold White, to deal with anything that might accrue during his absence, set off for the land of colour and sunshine. And now he was back.

He drove to Portland Place, after arranging at the station for his heavier luggage to be sent on, and was greeted with delight by his small household, which had been apprised of his arrival by telegram. A cheerful fire burned in the study; and looking round the cosy, familiar room, Lowe nodded with satisfaction.

'It's good to be back,' he said simply. 'Anything of interest been happening while I was away?'

Arnold White gave an account of all that had occurred. The management of the Pantheon Theatre wanted a new play — two film companies were in need of scenarios . . . The dramatist listened while he sipped the coffee which his house-keeper had hastily prepared.

'And,' White concluded with a smile, 'I think Shadgold is rather keen to see you.'

'Oh, what does he want?' asked Lowe, raising his eyebrows.

The secretary made a grimace. 'What does he always want? Haven't you been reading your newspapers?'

The dramatist shook his head. 'No, I haven't seen a newspaper for nearly three weeks. You must remember that I was ordered away for a rest.'

'Then you've missed these 'Bell' murders. It's the most extraordinary thing — ' He broke off as there came a tap at the door and the housekeeper entered.

'Detective-Inspector Shadgold's called, sir,' she said indignantly. 'It's too bad! He's hardly given you time to get inside the place. Shall I tell 'im you aren't in?'

Lowe shook his head. 'No, no. Ask the inspector in at once.'

The housekeeper departed reluctantly, and presently Shadgold came into the room with an outstretched hand. 'Glad to

21

see you back, Mr. Lowe,' he greeted, throwing his hard derby hat on to the settee. 'Hope the holiday's done you good. You look pretty well, I must say.'

'I feel pretty well, Shadgold,' answered the dramatist.

'Wish I could say the same,' sighed the inspector. 'I may as well tell you right away that this isn't only a friendly visit.'

'What's the trouble?' asked Lowe, slowly filling his pipe.

'Trouble enough,' was the gloomy answer. 'There's been a devil at work while you've been away, Mr. Lowe, and I'd give half my pension to lay him by the heels!'

'Sit down and let's hear all about it.' The dramatist nodded towards an armchair. 'Give Inspector Shadgold a cigar and a drink, will you, White?' he added, and the secretary obeyed.

When the whisky was sizzling in a glass at his elbow and he had lighted his cigar, the inspector leaned back in his chair and rubbed at his stiff moustache. 'I won't go into all the details, Mr. Lowe,' he began. 'You can find those out from records. The main point is that there have been four murders in just over a month and there isn't the ghost of a clue as to who did them. Nothing! Except that in each case a little silver bell was left on the body of the victim.'

An expression of interest came into Lowe's eyes. 'A silver bell, eh?' he remarked, applying a lighted match to the bowl of his pipe and puffing thoughtfully. 'What kind of a bell?'

'The sort of thing you can get in any toyshop or stores where they cater for children,' answered Shadgold. 'The kind of trumpery little decoration you use on a Christmas tree.'

'Extraordinary!' Lowe leaned back in his chair and blew a trumpet of smoke ceiling-wards. 'Go on, I'm interested, Shadgold. Tell me all about it.'

As briefly as possible Shadgold complied.

'I've got to do something and I'm hanged if I know what!' he concluded. 'The newspapers are beginning to say some nasty things about the Yard, and the assistant commissioner's in the devil of a temper. Of course, as usual, I get the brunt of it.'

'And there's no connection whatever between the victims?' asked Lowe, his eyes on the ceiling.

'Not the slightest!' declared the inspector, shaking his bullet head. 'That's the first thing we looked for, naturally, and we can't find the remotest link between any of them. They were four people as wide apart in their interests as anybody you could find who spoke the same language.'

That the dramatist was interested was obvious from his face.

'So, at the moment,' he remarked, after a slight pause, 'the only clue you've got are these bells which were pinned to the coats of the murdered men?'

'That's all,' grunted Shadgold. 'And a fat lot of good that is. You see, Mr. Lowe, they weren't even killed in the same way. Usually a maniac, when he goes in for killing on a large scale, uses the same methods every time.'

'Do you seriously suggest this is the work of a maniac?'

There was something in his tone that

caused the detective to redden. 'What else can anyone think?' he asked defensively. 'There doesn't seem to be any rhyme or reason for the crimes. The theory at the Yard is that there is a homicidal maniac at large — and the sooner we catch him, the better for all concerned.'

Lowe pursed his lips doubtfully. 'I don't want to pass an opinion until I've read the reports,' he said, 'but I'm always inclined to discount this lunatic theory. It's such an easy way out. Of course, you may be right. A homicidal maniac is not unknown in the annals of crime, but I think we should exhaust every other explanation before we consider that as a solution.'

'I've exhausted most of 'em,' said Shadgold wearily. 'Perhaps you'll be luckier, Mr. Lowe.' He rose to his feet. 'I've brought everything that's known about the business with me.' He jerked his head towards a parcel which he had brought in with him.

Lowe's eyes twinkled. 'You seem to have been pretty certain I'd help,' he murmured.

Shadgold looked uncomfortable. 'Well

— I hoped — I thought — ' he mumbled incoherently.

'And you were right,' broke in the dramatist. 'I'm intensely interested.'

'I hope you'll be able to spot something that we've overlooked,' said Shadgold, jamming his bowler hat firmly on his head and holding out his hand.

'I'll certainly do my best.'

'I'll get along then, Mr. Lowe. I've got a conference at the Yard in twenty minutes. Nothing but conferences these days,' he added grumblingly, and took his departure.

When he had gone, Lowe opened the parcel and scanned through the typewritten reports and statements it contained. They were many and various and he settled back in his chair with the pleasurable anticipation of several hours' enjoyment.

It was a long time since Shadgold had brought him a problem to tackle, and this promised, from the little he had heard of it, to be just the type of puzzle he liked.

4

Gloria Swayne's Story

He had barely finished reading through the mass of material relevant to the four crimes when his housekeeper tapped and entered hesitantly.

'I'm sorry to disturb you, sir,' she apologised, 'but there's a young woman who practically insists on seeing you. I told her you was busy, but she wouldn't go away until I'd given you her card.'

She presented a salver on which lay a slip of pasteboard, and Lowe took it. His eyebrows went up as he read the name that was neatly engraved on the card.

'You may ask Miss Swayne to come in,' he said.

'Are you going to see her?'

'Certainly I'm going to see her,' he answered curtly.

'If you goes on like this,' said the motherly woman, 'we shall be 'aving you ill again. You 'aven't been 'ome ten minutes, in the manner of speaking, and people comes buzzing round the place like flies round a jam-pot.'

'I don't feel in the least like a jam-pot,' said Lowe good-humouredly. 'Now go and ask Miss Swayne to come in, there's a good soul.'

The housekeeper departed, her homely face clouded, and the dramatist stared at the card he still held in his hand.

It was an extraordinary coincidence, this visit from the woman who had been mixed up with the first murder that signalised the coming of the bells. He knew her slightly — she had played in one of his films — and he had been considering calling on her. And now she had come to him. What had she come for? Was her visit concerned with the death of Richard Sinclair, or had she come in connection with some other business?

He rose as the door opened and Gloria Swayne was ushered in; and as he turned to greet her, he noticed that her lovely face was pale and haggard. There was no doubt that she deserved the flattering descriptions that so often appeared in the newspapers concerning her. To her natural beauty was added a grace of figure and poise that many women would have envied. Even now, with the violet shadows that circled the wide blue eyes, the pale sunken cheeks, and the general air of strain and nervousness, she was sufficiently above the average to warrant a second glance in a crowd of normally pretty women.

'Good afternoon, Miss Swayne,' he said pleasantly as she stood hesitantly in the doorway.

'Good afternoon, Mr. Lowe,' she replied, and her voice was low and musical, a voice which even the blaring distortion of the average cinema loudspeaker could not render entirely unpleasant. 'I hope you'll forgive me for bothering you, but I — I want your advice.'

'That's easily given,' said the dramatist, pushing forward a chair. 'Won't you sit down.'

'Thank you.' She came further into the room. 'I remembered that you — that you were interested in crime and I — I didn't want to go to the police . . . '

So she had come about Sinclair's death, thought Lowe. 'You're lucky to find me at home,' he said. 'I've only just got back from Spain.'

'I know.' She sank into the chair, and her fingers played nervously with her handbag. It was some time before she spoke again, and he waited patiently.

'Mr. Lowe,' she said suddenly, 'I'm afraid! That's why I've come to you today. Since that — that terrible morning when poor Richard was killed, I've gone in fear of my life!'

He looked at her in genuine astonishment. 'In fear of your life?' he repeated slowly.

'Yes,' she said huskily. 'I'm afraid — I'm afraid I may be the next one! I'm afraid that any moment may be my last! I'm afraid to eat or drink, even to walk in the street!' Her voice shook, and there was terror in the eyes that looked up at him.

'Are you sure,' he said kindly, 'that you aren't alarming yourself unnecessarily? Have you any concrete reason to suppose that there's a chance of your — being killed?'

'Yes, there's a very real reason. I believe that — that these crimes are directed at me! I believe that I'm partly, if not wholly, responsible for the deaths of these — these four men!'

During the course of his eventful life, Trevor Lowe had suffered many surprises, but this was by far the greatest he had ever experienced. Was this woman suffering from a delusion? Had the strain of the studio murder so affected her nerves that she had begun to imagine something that had no basis in fact?

'Suppose you tell me what grounds you have for your supposition?' he suggested, seating himself opposite her.

'What I'm going to tell you started four years ago,' she began nervously, mechanically taking off her gloves as she spoke. 'I was then practically an unknown actress. I'd played in the chorus for some time, and there didn't seem the least chance of my reaching anything better. The struggles and disappointments that I endured have nothing to do with this matter, and therefore I shall not go into them, but — well, you know the stage, Mr. Lowe; you know how difficult it is to become a success.'

She paused and moistened her lips.

'It was one night at the theatre — we were playing in Manchester at the time,' she went on, 'that I had a visitor. A card was sent round to me bearing the name Nottingham Deane, and scrawled on the back was the request that if I could spare a moment, I should hear something very much to my advantage. I hesitated, and then agreed to see this unknown visitor. It is not an uncommon occurrence, as you know; for men to try, on some pretext or other, to get acquainted with stage women — ' She smiled rather wanly. ' — and I thought this might be just an excuse for meeting me. But my doubts were soon to be dispelled. The man who was shown into my dressing room was as unlike the usual stage-door lounger as it's possible to imagine, for during the whole of the ensuing conversation I never once saw his face.'

'You never saw his face?' said the dramatist as she paused.

'No.' She shook her head. 'He kept a silk muffler he was wearing close up over his mouth and nostrils so that only his eyes were visible.'

'Extraordinary!' murmured Lowe. 'Go on, Miss Swayne.'

'I won't repeat the interview in detail,' she continued, 'but the upshot of the conversation was that he was convinced I had a great screen personality and only needed a chance to bring it out. I must admit I was a little sceptical, because I'd heard pretty much the same thing from a number of other people who were prepared to put me at the top of my profession for — a consideration.' Her lips curled cynically. 'However, again I was wrong, for he finally made a proposal that left me gasping. He said he would put the sum of fifty thousand pounds to my credit and undertake to provide me with the leading part in a big film then going into production, if I'd agree to remain unmarried for a period of five years.

'My first conviction was that he was a madman; but when he produced, then and there, a thousand pounds in notes, I had to reconsider this first impression. I agreed to meet him after the show was over and go further into the matter.

'To be perfectly candid, Mr. Lowe, I never expected him to turn up. But when I came out just after eleven, there was a huge saloon car drawn up outside the passage that led to the stage door, and my unknown visitor was waiting for me. We drove for about ten miles, as near as I could calculate, finally halting in the drive of a gloomy old house standing well back from the road; and during the whole journey my companion never uttered a word.

'I was hurried inside the house, feeling by this time rather nervous, with my brain in a whirl, and taken into a heavily curtained room where two men were sitting. They were introduced to me as Mr. Smith and Mr. Jones, although I suspected that these were very far from being their right names. One of them produced a document in which was set out a statement that I would, in consideration of the sum of fifty thousand pounds and the leading part in a new film, *Women of the Dust*, agree to remain unmarried for a period of five years from that date. If at any time I broke my agreement, then I was willing to accept whatever punishment Mr. Nottingham Deane saw fit to impose.'

She stopped to recover her breath, but the dramatist made no comment, waiting for her to continue her extraordinary story. 'Perhaps I was mad,' she said, 'to even think of signing such a document; but the truth of the matter is, Mr. Lowe, I would have signed anything to have got out of that house. The atmosphere frightened me. I can't explain why, but I was terrified. I signed, and two days later I received two letters: one from the Manchester branch of the London and Counties Bank saying that the sum of fifty thousand pounds had been deposited to my credit, and the other from English Films Limited offering me the leading part in their next picture, *Women of the Dust*. The mysterious Mr. Deane had apparently kept his word, and since I had signed an agreement to that effect I had to keep mine.'

The low voice in which she had carried

on her conversation grew husky.

'It isn't generally known, but Dick — Mr. Sinclair — and I were engaged. Mr. Shuberg knew it, but otherwise it was a secret. We were — were tremendously attached to one another, so much so that I was even contemplating marrying him in spite of the agreement I had made.

'Two days before his death, I received a message, just a typewritten sheet of paper with the words 'Remember your promise' signed with the initials N.D.'

'You have this paper?' asked Lowe quickly.

She nodded, and fumbling in her bag produced a crumpled slip which she handed to him. He looked at it. There was no name, date nor address; only the message she had mentioned typewritten across the centre.

'May I keep this?' he asked, and she consented.

'What about the other three men?' he went on, folding the paper and putting it in his pocket. 'What connection did they have with you?'

She smiled a little ruefully. 'Mr. Jones was just an admirer. Rather a persistent admirer, I must admit. He used to write me the most plaintive letters saying how much he — he loved me, and begging me to see him. Solomon Riess was merely a great friend. He knew me when I was a little girl and used to take me about a great deal. He was a splendid dancer, and I liked to dance with him, but there was nothing more. The poor undertaker at Hendon once wrote to me asking for a photograph, saying that he had been so impressed by a performance of mine that he couldn't get me out of his mind. I sent him one, and in answer received a proposal of marriage. Naturally I didn't reply to it. I — I get quite a number of letters in the same strain, and it's better not to take any notice of them. Now I'm afraid to be seen with anyone in case — in case I'm signing their death warrant. It's terrible!'

Her voice cracked, and Lowe looked at her gravely. There was no doubt that this woman's nerves were in shreds. It was visible in her eyes and in the nervous shaking of her hands.

'You've said nothing about this to the

police?' he enquired.

'I have said nothing about it to anybody,' she answered. 'Dick knew — about the contract I mean — but no one else.'

'And you only saw this man Deane once?' he enquired.

'Only once,' she replied. 'I've never seen him before or since.'

'And these two men who were introduced to you as Mr. Smith and Mr. Jones, what were they like?'

She considered for a little while before replying.

'One was rather thin,' she said presently, 'and the other was thick-set and of a stoutish build. They were both clean-shaven, but beyond that I'm afraid I was too nervous to notice much about them.'

Lowe pursed his lips. The description was so vague as to be useless for the purposes of identification. 'It's the most extraordinary story I've ever listened to,' he declared truthfully. 'I don't quite know how to advise you, Miss Swayne, and that's candid. If what you say is true, and I don't doubt it for the moment, you certainly seem to be in some kind of danger. For the present, I would suggest you stay at home as much as possible, cancel all your engagements, and be seen with nobody who's likely to arouse the antagonism of the illusive and mysterious Nottingham Deane. In the meantime, I'll see if I can find out what's behind that extraordinary contract.'

'It's very good of you — ' she began gratefully.

'Nothing of the sort,' interrupted Lowe. 'I'm intensely interested; the more so since my friend, Inspector Shadgold, has already asked me to help him over these bell murders. Really, I'm the one who should be grateful to you.'

She smiled and got up slowly. 'That's a very nice way of putting it,' she said. 'But I do thank you all the same for having listened to me so sympathetically. I feel much better now that I've told you.' She held out a small hand and he took it.

'Before you go,' he said, 'what was the name of the theatre you were playing at in Manchester when you first saw this man, Nottingham Deane?'

'The Grand. I believe it's a picture house now.'

'One more thing,' he said as he made a note of her reply. 'Will you send me the card that Deane sent to you, if you still have it, and a copy of the agreement?'

'I never had a copy of the agreement, but I've still got the card. I'll send it round as soon as I get home.'

He accompanied her to the door of the flat and came back to the study, his brows drawn together. The story Gloria Swayne had told him required a lot of reflection, and he was still pondering over it when Arnold White came in.

'Wasn't that Gloria Swayne, the film star, who just left?' he enquired.

Lowe nodded.

'What did she want to see you for?' asked the secretary, and he pursed his lips in a low whistle when his employer explained. 'I suppose she was telling the truth?' he remarked.

'I see no reason why she shouldn't have been,' answered the dramatist. 'She impressed me as being serious.'

'You must admit it's a queer story,' said

White doubtfully.

'Queer, but very interesting,' murmured Lowe. He had picked up a timetable from his desk and was rapidly turning the pages. 'I've got a job for you,' he said. 'There's a train for Manchester that leaves Euston in an hour. I want you to catch it. Find out the name of the stage-door keeper who worked at the Grand Theatre four years ago and see if he remembers anything of Mr. Nottingham Deane. You can phone me the result of your enquiries.'

Arnold White, who liked nothing better than these incursions into crime which since the Carroway affair had become increasingly frequent, nodded.

'In the meantime,' the dramatist went on, 'I have one or two ideas of my own that may or may not lead to something. Keep in touch with me, and if I should be out, leave a message.'

The secretary hurried away to prepare for his journey, and neither he nor Lowe realised that that journey heralded the beginning of as difficult and dangerous a task as any they had ever tackled.

5

The Providence Mission

There were many people in the East End of London who had cause to bless the name of Mr. Jonathan Grandsire. It was eight or nine years since he had come quietly and without ostentation to settle in a quiet street near Stepney Station, and to open what he subsequently called The Providence Mission, but which became known in the district colloquially as The Prov. Here the relatives of convicted men, and all those who had fallen by the wayside, could come for succour without fear of being turned away. The only stipulation was that the relatives themselves should be guiltless of crime, whatever their men- or women-folk might have done.

It is to be regretted, however, that Mr. Grandsire was a somewhat gullible man and could never resist an appeal, provided it was couched cleverly enough; and the people who took advantage of his good nature were many and varied. His charity was given to the most undeserving at times; and although in fairness to the majority of those he helped, it must be admitted that they deserved it, there were numerous others who preyed upon this good man, receiving his beneficence under false pretences.

He had bought up three houses that had been condemned by the local council, and turned them into one long low structure with a common dining-room running the length of the building. Upstairs were a number of bedrooms and one dormitory wherein those who were destitute might pass the night, or even longer, if their position was acute and they could satisfy Mr. Grandsire of their bona-fides.

He was a man of about sixty with white hair and the rosy face of a countryman. He affected a certain primness of dress, but the primness of a past generation; and wore on most occasions an old-fashioned Norfolk suit with the pockets bulging with sweets which during his walks abroad he would distribute to the children of the neighbourhood.

His help at the Prov consisted of a cook, a boy of sixteen, and a doorkeeper, whose duty it was to ascertain the genuineness of the numerous clients who required assistance. 'Cosh' Willis was an ex-convict who had served several long terms for robbery with violence and had been one of Mr. Grandsire's earliest converts. That benevolent old gentleman was never tired of relating how he had saved this particular brand from the burning, but it must be admitted that the contributory cause was the fact that Cosh had been promised the cat for his next offence, and a stiff sentence as a habitual criminal. At the Prov he had an easy berth, and was not averse to a little knocking off whenever he got a chance.

The local police did not at first take kindly to these activities on the part of Mr. Grandsire; but realising that nobody could possibly take offence at such a harmless old gentleman, they allowed him to carry on his work unmolested, contenting themselves with keeping a watchful eye on the various people who passed in and out of the mission, and occasionally making an official inspection of the place.

There was one bright spot in Mr. Grandsire's grey and rather lonely life, and that was his adopted son, Ronald. Shortly after he had come to Stepney, Mr. Grandsire had been awakened one night by the sound of irregular sobbing outside his window. Going down to the rainy street to discover the cause, he had found a small boy, about fourteen years of age, wet through and shivering with cold, huddled on the doorstep. He had taken the lad in, warmed and fed him, and made enquiries which had elicited the fact that his parents were both in prison and that the child had been left homeless to fend for himself. Touched by his plight and evident misery, Mr. Grandsire had, with his habitual kindness, taken him under his wing, and upon the death of his parents had legally adopted him. He had sent him to a good school, and on his leaving had articled him to a firm of solicitors in the City. And now the one-time waif was on the verge of passing his final examinations.

The story had spread round the district with remarkable rapidity, and the inhabitants were very well disposed towards Ronald, mainly because his legal knowledge was of great assistance to them in their continual fight with the law.

On the day following Trevor Lowe's interview with Gloria Swayne, the young man came into the little office where his foster-father worked. The old man looked up as the slim, athletic figure entered and smiled affectionately.

'Hello, Ronald!' he said, a note of pleasure in his voice. 'It's unusual for you to come at this hour of the day. I didn't expect to see you until this evening.'

At his express desire, his adopted son did not live with him. The old man contended that the atmosphere of Stepney was unsuitable; and as soon as Ronald had been old enough to look after himself, he had taken a flat for him in the neighbourhood of Kingsway, which was within easy distance of the office of the solicitor's where he worked.

'I had to come down this way on business,' said Ronald, pulling up a chair and sitting down, 'so I thought I'd drop in for a moment.'

'I'm very pleased to see you, my boy,' said Mr. Grandsire, leaning back in his chair. 'Very pleased.'

Ronald Lane — Grandsire had insisted at the time of the adoption that he should keep his own name — lighted a cigarette and looked at his benefactor through the smoke nervously.

'Well, what is it?' said Mr. Grandsire good-humouredly. 'Come along, out with it; you've got something you want to tell me?'

'Is it as obvious as that?' Ronald smiled. 'Well, as a matter of fact, I have.'

'What is it?' enquired the elder man; and then, as Ronald hesitated: 'You haven't been getting into any sort of trouble, have you?'

'No, no; it's not that!'

The cloud passed from his face as his son hastened to reassure him.

'It's — you'll probably think I'm an

awful fool — but — ' he stammered incoherently, and reddened.

Mr. Grandsire raised his grey eyebrows. 'You seem to find it very difficult,' he remarked.

Ronald fidgeted uneasily. 'It isn't easy,' he confessed after a pause. 'I'm so afraid that — that you'll laugh at me.'

The kind eyes of the old man were very soft as he looked at his adopted son. 'Have you ever found me unsympathetic?' he asked gently.

Ronald shook his head. 'No, but — now that I've come to put the thing into words, it seems a little silly, even to me.'

'Suppose you tell me all about it?'

'Well, the fact of the matter is, Dad . . . ' Ronald screwed up his courage and took the plunge. 'I've — I've met a woman. I told you you'd laugh!' he added as the other smiled.

'I'm not laughing,' said Mr. Grandsire. 'I've been wondering how long it would be before something of the sort happened. Who is the lucky young lady?'

'She's — she's — ' Ronald's nervousness came flooding back. 'Well, you'll say it's ridiculous, of course. She's rather a famous person.'

'Well, perhaps you'll be a famous person one day.'

'But she's very famous,' stammered Ronald. 'It — it's Gloria Swayne, the film actress!'

'Gloria Swayne!' The words came from the old man's lips jerkily, and he stared at his son as though he had seen a ghost. 'Gloria Swayne, of all people! How did you come to meet her, boy?'

Ronald was too absorbed in his own thoughts to notice the change of tone and expression. 'She's a client of ours,' he explained, 'and I've had to go round several times to see her on business for the firm. Dad, she's wonderful! I've never seen anyone so lovely before in my life!'

There was a long silence, and then the old man spoke. 'There are many women in England,' he said adjusting his glasses, 'and out of that number you had to choose the one woman who will bring you misery and unhappiness!'

His son stared at him in consternation. 'What do you mean? There's — there's nothing wrong with her, is there?'

'There's nothing wrong with any woman until you know her,' answered his foster-father. 'Forget this nonsense, my boy! When it's time for you to marry, find yourself a nice homely wife, but think no more of Gloria Swayne!'

Ronald's face clouded. 'I didn't think you'd take it that way, Dad,' he muttered grumpily. 'After all, I don't suppose I've got an earthly chance — '

'Let's hope you haven't!' said the old man sternly. 'You may think I'm hard, Ronald; but, believe me, I have only your happiness at heart — and happiness and Gloria Swayne do not go together. That woman is poisonous!'

The young man's face set stubbornly. 'You're prejudiced because she's an actress — ' he began, but Mr. Grandsire stopped him with a gesture.

'I'm not!' he answered. 'I have nothing against actresses.'

'Then why do you say she's poisonous?'

'I have my reasons. Very good reasons, which I should prefer not to tell you. I

50

don't blame you for being attracted to her, that's only natural — but put her out of your mind, my boy, and forget this nonsense!'

'If you'll give me a good reason,' said Ronald, but again the other interrupted him.

'I shall give you no other reason than that I think further acquaintance with Gloria Swayne is bad for you,' he said, his usually gentle voice harsh. 'That must be sufficient!'

'I think you're being very unreasonable!' protested Ronald. 'And very unjust. If I'd thought you were going to take it like this, I would never have told you. After all, as I say, I don't suppose she'd look at me for one moment. In her eyes I'm just a lawyer's clerk, and although she's been very gracious, our relations are purely business ones.'

'Keep them so,' said Mr. Grandsire. 'Keep them so, Ronald. Fond as I am of you, I would rather see you dead than married to that woman!'

'But why? What do you know about her? It's unfair to make these accusations

51

unless you're prepared to substantiate them!'

'I've made no accusations. I've only warned you. Come, Ronald,' he added less harshly, 'we've never quarrelled before, so let's not start now. There's a wide gulf separating you and Gloria Swayne, a gulf that will probably never be bridged, so why should we allow an unlikely possibility to come between us?'

Ronald's face cleared and he smiled wryly. 'There's a lot of truth in that, Dad,' he said. 'Let's say nothing more about it.'

For a quarter of an hour they chatted about other things; but Mr. Grandsire, who had made a study of his fellow men, knew that beneath his adopted son's apparent acceptance of the situation still lurked a faint resentment. For the first time, a barrier had crept up between them.

Ronald had to return to his office, and could not stay very long. For some time after he had taken his leave, his foster-father sat at his desk, staring in front of him, a stern expression on his usually genial face.

He was sitting thus when there came a tap on the door and the battered features of Mr. Willis peered into the room.

'There's a bloke wot wants to see yer, guv'nor,' he said in a half whisper. ''E looks like a busy to me.'

The old man looked up with a sigh. 'Let him come in, Willis,' he said, 'and don't be so secretive. We have nothing to hide from the police. They're as free to come and go here as the air.'

Cosh sniffed. 'All right, have it your own way,' he said disapprovingly. 'Shall I send 'im in, then?'

Mr. Grandsire nodded, and the ex-convict withdrew.

The man who presently entered the office was, contrary to the estimate of Mr. Willis, not a detective, and would have been indignant had he imagined that he had been mistaken as belonging to such a despised calling. In that overcrowded department at Scotland Yard which housed the records of convicted criminals, his dossier occupied a considerable space.

'Come in,' said Mr. Grandsire, and he pointed to a chair.

The newcomer sat down, and the old man went over and locked the door.

'Well . . . ' he said, returning to his desk; and the conversation that followed would have been of interest to a great many people, and particularly to Inspector Shadgold, had he been there to overhear what was being said.

6

The House in Hulme Road

Arnold white arrived at the Midland Station in Manchester late in the evening and discovered that the city was living up to its reputation, for rain was falling heavily, and a clammy air of depression hung over the gloomy town.

Coming out of the station, he hailed a taxi, telling the man to drive to the Grand Theatre. The cab moved off through the murky streets and presently drew up before an imposing frontage, the glittering lights of which were reflected blearily in the streaming pavement. White got out and eyed the exhibition of lurid posters that plastered the walls.

'Is this the place that used to be a theatre about four years ago?' he asked as he paid the driver.

The man nodded. 'This is the place,' he grunted, looking at the coins in his palm with satisfaction. 'Bit different to what it is now, though. A dirty, dingy old place it used to be.'

With a grinding of gears, the cab moved off into the falling rain; and after a quick glance round, White walked towards a little alley he could see running down by the side of the building. As he expected, he presently came to an aged sign with the words 'Stage Door' in faded letters.

Evidently the people who had taken over the building and converted it into a cinema had not considered it necessary to redecorate the rear portion. The narrow door below the sign was open, and entering the little passageway beyond, White rapped on a glass window that screened a cubbyhole on the right.

The old and not very clean face of a man appeared from somewhere and peered out at him. 'What d'you want?' asked a cracked, husky voice.

'Are you the doorkeeper?' asked White.

'Yus,' was the curt reply.

'I'd like a word with you. Were you here four years ago?'

The old man's water, red-rimmed eyes

regarded him suspiciously. 'Four years?' he repeated. 'Aye, and fifteen years afore that. What do you want to know for?'

'Because I'm in search of some information I think you could give me.'

The suspicion in the faded eyes deepened. 'Maybe I can, maybe I can't,' was the uncompromising reply.

'At least you can try,' suggested Arnold persuasively. His hand came out of his pocket and played ostentatiously with a pound note.

'Maybe I can,' agreed the old man, his small eyes fixed on the note greedily. 'Better come inside, where I can 'ear better.'

He pulled open a narrow door, and White entered the tiny office, redolent with the stale fumes of strong tobacco and decorated with hundreds of fly-marked photographs of past celebrities.

'Sit 'e down,' said the doorkeeper, pointing to a broken chair. 'Now, what is it yer want to know?'

Arnold perched himself on the edge of the rickety piece of furniture and explained. The old man's wrinkled forehead puckered up until he resembled a wizened and ancient monkey.

'I recoiled the feller,' he said slowly. "E was a party in h'evenin' dress, and 'e were all muffled up so that 'is face were 'id. Give me a five-pound note to take 'is card to a young lady in the chorus, 'e did. Yes, I recollect 'im very well indeed. Five-pounds notes weren't plentiful in them days — any more than they is now,' he added sorrowfully.

'Could you describe this man?' asked the secretary eagerly.

The doorkeeper pursed his lips and scratched his chin. 'Can't rightly say as I could,' he answered thoughtfully. "E was a toff, you could see that, but there weren't much of 'is face to be seen. I remember it struck me at the time that 'e didn't *want* it ter be seen.'

White gave no sign of the disappointment he felt. So far the only result of his journey had been to bear out Gloria Swayne's story, at least, up to a point.

'Have you ever seen him before?' he persisted.

The man shook his grizzled head

slowly. 'No, I never seen 'im before. And I ain't never seen 'im since. I could tell you one thing, though — when 'e pulled out the five-pound note to give me, 'e dropped an envelope from 'is pocket, and there was a name on it. I found it after 'e'd gone, and I recollect I waited to see 'im again to return it to 'im, but 'e never come back.'

Here was something, thought White. If the man had dropped an envelope, it was more than likely it had contained his name and address on it. People did not, as a rule, carry letters that were not their own about with them.

'Do you remember what the name was?' he asked.

'No, I don't,' said the doorkeeper, 'but I can find out for you, I've still got that there envelope. I remember I kep' it for a long time, and I believe it's still amongst some odds and ends in my lodgings.'

Here was an unexpected piece of luck. The mysterious Mr. Nottingham Deane had left behind something that might very likely prove a clue to his real identity, for it was pretty evident that the name he had given to Gloria Swayne was not his own.

'I'd like to see that envelope,' said White.

'If I've still got it, you can,' answered the other, 'but you'll 'ave to come round to my diggin's. I'll be 'ome about a quarter past eleven, so if you pop round then I'll see if I can find it. Twenty-three Hulme Road, the address is, an' ask for Taverner — that's my name,' he added unnecessarily.

'I'll come round about twelve,' said White, slipping the note into Mr. Taverner's hand. He cut short the doorkeeper's questions as to what it was all about, and hurrying up the little passageway came out into the main road, feeling not a little pleased with his evening's work. Something, at any rate, had been done, and perhaps he was on the verge of a discovery that would prove to be important.

A man who had been staring intently at one of the posters in front of the cinema watched him out of the corner of his eye, and turning away began to follow leisurely in his wake. Unconscious of his trailer, Arnold White made his way to a hotel and booked a room. He had still nearly two hours to put in before he could keep his appointment with Mr. Taverner, and he occupied part of the time by telephoning to Portland Place, only to learn from the housekeeper that Lowe was out and was not expected back until very late.

He filled in the rest of the time by having supper, and then set out to find Hulme Road. The rain had ceased, but the air was still damp and cold, and a thin mist added to the general unpleasantness.

It took him some time to find Mr. Taverner's lodgings, and it was a quarter to twelve before he succeeded in discovering the narrow street which lay in a dingy district at the back of the cinema. Number twenty-three was an exact replica of all the other houses in the ugly thoroughfare. The front door opened directly onto the pavement, and after assuring himself that he was at the right house by glancing at the shining brass numbers that had been screwed on the blistered portal, he knocked.

He had barely taken his hand from the knocker when a window opened above him and the husky voice of a man enquired his business.

'I want to see Mr. Taverner,' said White. 'He said he'd be home at this time.'

'Wait a minute,' grunted the voice, and the window was slammed.

There was a slight delay, and then he heard the shuffle of footsteps and the front door opened. A dim figure loomed in the blackness of the passage beyond.

'Come in, will you,' said the voice of the man who had spoken from the window a few seconds earlier, and Arnold White stepped over the threshold.

As he did so, something came down on his head with crushing force. A sharp pain seared through his brain, and he collapsed into a crumpled heap at the feet of the man who had struck him down.

7

The Undertaker's Hobby

Trevor Lowe spent the greater part of the afternoon following his secretary's departure in thinking over the facts in his possession and evolving a line of action. It was a puzzling problem, and Gloria Swayne's visit had contributed nothing towards the solution. If anything, it had added to the mystery. Who was Nottingham Deane, and what had been his object in suggesting that Gloria should sign that very strange document? And what connection did it have with the silver bell murders?

The woman's fear was understandable, but Lowe found himself unable to accept her suggestion that it was because they had evinced an interest in her that these four men had been killed. No one, unless they were mentally unhinged, would go to such lengths as murder in order to enforce a clause in a contract. Apart from which, with the exception of Richard Sinclair, there was no likelihood of her marrying any of the victims. If that contract, signed in the lonely house ten miles outside Manchester four years ago, had anything to do with the more recent crimes, there was something deeper behind it. But much as he tried, the dramatist could find no reasonable suggestion.

He had gone carefully through the evidence at his disposal a second time, and there was nothing which had come to light to remotely connect the four victims of the unknown killer.

Scotland Yard had gone very carefully into this question, for it seemed the most obvious starting point; yet the result of their enquiries revealed no association whatever between the popular star, the retired grocer, the Hatton Garden diamond merchant, and the unfortunate undertaker. So far as this was concerned, Lowe thought it could be accepted as a fact. If there had been anything between these men, the police would have discovered it. In that kind of enquiry, they were without compare.

Putting aside the possibility that the whole thing was the work of a maniac — and Lowe, as he had told Shadgold, was not prepared to consider this until every other supposition had failed — what possible motive could lie behind the affair? Admitting for the sake of argument that that extraordinary contract of Gloria Swayne's was part and parcel of the silver bell mystery, did it help to render it any clearer?

After half an hour's concentrated thought, Lowe was forced to admit that it didn't. Here was an unknown woman who had been travelling in a second-rate touring company in the chorus. One night, without any reason, an offer is made to her consisting of fifty thousand pounds in cash and the leading part in a new film, providing that she undertakes not to marry for a period of five years. The man who puts up this proposition takes the greatest pains to conceal his identity, and is never seen again. Four years afterward, four men more or less acquainted with the woman who has now become a star are murdered, and pinned to the lapels of their coats in each instance is a little silver bell.

The thing was preposterous! There was neither rhyme nor reason, so far as Lowe could see. There was not even any concrete evidence to show that the contract and the deaths of these men had anything in common. There was no starting point. It was useless going over the ground already covered by the police, and he failed to see any point from which he could begin his enquiries.

It was true that White's expedition might result in something. Perhaps if this mysterious Nottingham Deane could be traced, his identity might throw a new light on the matter. But the probability was remote that the doorkeeper, even if he was still alive and White could locate him, would be in a position to help. Four years was a long time, and it was doubtful if the man would remember anything of importance. However, it had been the obvious line to take, and there was nothing for it but to hope for the best.

In the meanwhile, until he heard from

his secretary, Lowe decided to pursue a line of enquiry which had suggested itself to him.

In reading through the reports concerning the death of the undertaker, he had noticed that a witness at the inquest had stated in evidence that the dead man — his name was Bookham — had had a queer hobby. He collected the newspaper accounts of murder trials. The police had apparently not considered this fact of sufficient importance to follow up, for there was no further mention of it in the reports Shadgold had brought. The dramatist, however, considered that it was worth looking into. It was not that he expected it to yield any striking results, but he thought it might possibly suggest something that would open up a new line of enquiry; and since his material was so very meagre, he concluded that anything that added to it was of value. It might be purely a waste of time, and on the other hand it might not; and when he had finished his tea, he set off to Hendon and the house of the witness who had mentioned Mr. Bookham's strange amusement.

This gentleman kept a draper's shop close to the establishment of the unfortunate undertaker. Mr. Meek, like Bookham had been, was a bachelor, and the two had been close friends. The drapery emporium was closed when the dramatist reached Hendon, but he succeeded in tracking its proprietor to his private residence, a small neat house in a row of other small neat houses, and was received by Mr. Meek with eager nervousness.

The draper was a little man, and his business had so stamped him that it was not difficult to imagine the counter at which he spent the greater part of his time. He blinked at Lowe through a pair of powerful pince-nez and twisted his bony hands together as though he were about to sell him a bargain line in dress material.

'Poor Bookham — a dreadful thing!' he said in a thin piping voice, shaking his partially bald head. 'A dreadful thing! I knew him intimately. Of course, I'm willing to do anything I possibly can to help the cause of justice, but I told everything I knew at the inquest.'

'What I've come to talk to you about,' said Lowe, crossing his legs — they were sitting in Mr. Meek's austere little drawing-room — 'is concerned with your friend Bookham's hobby of collecting the newspaper accounts of murder trials.'

'Ah, yes,' said Mr. Meek, nodding very quickly. 'A most curious, and if I may say so, a rather morbid amusement. I used to remonstrate with Bookham about it. I am myself an ardent collector of foreign stamps — in a small way, you understand; I cannot of course afford the — er — the more expensive variety. I managed once to get hold of a bargain — '

'I was wondering,' broke in Lowe hastily, in no mood to listen to Mr. Meek's bargain, 'whether this hobby of Mr. Bookham's could have had anything to do with his death.'

Mr. Meek pursed his lips and smoothed the ends of his moustache with a finger and thumb. 'In what way, sir?' he asked doubtfully.

The dramatist shrugged his shoulders. 'I haven't the least idea,' he said candidly. 'But you'll understand, Mr. Meek, that even the vaguest possibility must be followed up.'

The little man nodded portentously. 'Of course, of course,' he agreed. 'Though really, I fail to see how poor Bookham's collection of cuttings can assist you in any way.'

Lowe failed to see, either, but it was a habit of his to leave nothing untried; and to this he owed in a great measure his success in these enquiries which he occasionally undertook for Shadgold.

'Was it a large collection?' he asked.

'Fairly so. It occupies twelve volumes.'

Lowe raised his eyebrows. He had expected nothing so vast as this. 'He must have been accumulating it for a very long time,' he remarked.

'Oh, yes, a very long time. Over a period of twenty-four years, he told me once.'

'Have you any idea what started his interest in such a subject?'

Mr. Meek nodded. 'Yes; he was once connected with a sensational murder trial himself.'

The dramatist pricked up his ears. 'Oh,

he was, was he?' he said softly. 'As a witness, do you mean?'

'No,' replied Mr. Meek. 'He was on the jury.'

A little light crept into Lowe's eyes. Here was something that the police had overlooked; something that might very easily turn out to be of vital importance. 'What was the case?' he asked.

'I'm afraid I don't know,' Mr. Meek replied. 'I once tried to get Bookham to tell me, but he refused. It was a very sensational and unsavoury crime; that's all he'd say about it. I think,' he added, 'that it upset him a good deal. He was a disbeliever in capital punishment, and one of his reasons for amassing the reports of trials was to substantiate a theory he held that only in one case out of fifty was the person's guilt really proved. I'm rather in agreement with him. What are your views on the subject?'

Lowe had no wish to discuss the ethics of capital punishment at that moment. 'I presume these volumes containing Bookham's collection are still in existence?' he said, ignoring the question.

'Oh, yes. They're still at his house with his other possessions. He left everything to a nephew, his only relative, who I understand is on his way home from abroad. Would you care to see them? I have the keys of the premises, and his house is only a few doors away.'

'I should like to see them very much,' said the dramatist, and the little draper rose to his feet.

'If you will excuse me while I put on my hat and coat,' he said, and left the room.

While Lowe waited for his return, he thought over what he had just learned. Was the hunch which had brought him on what had appeared at first to be a wild goose chase going to yield results? Was there a clue to be found in this ancient collection of the dead man's? He felt more than a little hopeful.

Mr. Meek returned clad in a sedate black overcoat, and together they left the house.

The undertaker's abode was similar in every respect to the draper's. Mr. Meek opened the gate and led the way up the little crazy-paved path. With a key he took from his pocket, he opened the front door and they passed into the house.

The atmosphere was stuffy, and there was the close smell associated with a place that had been shut up and unused for a time. Mr. Meek pressed a switch and illumined the hall, opened a door on the right, and ushered his companion into a square apartment furnished as austerely as his own. When he had put on the light, he pointed to an old-fashioned glass-fronted bookcase that stood against one wall.

'There are the cuttings,' he said.

The dramatist went over and, opening the doors, looked at the row of red-covered volumes that, with the exception of one blank space, occupied a complete shelf.

'I thought you said there were twelve?' he remarked presently. 'There are only eleven here.'

'Only eleven!' exclaimed Mr. Meek shrilly. 'Surely you must be mistaken!'

'Count them for yourself,' said Lowe, and the little draper did so.

'You're quite right!' he muttered,

frowning. 'But there were twelve. What's happened to the other one?'

Lowe was silent. He could have given a shrewd guess. Someone, for reasons of their own, had removed one of the volumes of Mr. Bookham's collection; and the reason was obvious. It had been removed because it contained a clue to the identity of his murderer!

8

The Faceless Man

Arnold White came to his senses with an aching head and a feeling of acute nausea. At first he was so dazed that he could remember nothing; and then gradually, as the throbbing eased in his temples, he was able to recollect what had happened.

He remembered coming to the house and stepping into the darkened hall, and the avalanche that had descended on him. His limbs were stiff and cramped, and when he tried to move them he discovered that his ankles and hands were securely bound.

He was lying on his back on what seemed to be a pile of sacking that smelt mildewed and unpleasant. There was not the faintest glimmer of light anywhere, and he concluded that it must either be night time, or else he was in some room where there was no window. The former seemed the more reasonable supposition, since he could scarcely have been unconscious for long.

He listened, but he could hear no sound. After lying quietly until the pain in his head had almost ceased, he set about trying to find some way out of his predicament.

For several minutes he struggled with the cords at his wrists, and quickly found that the more he did so the tighter they became. He gave it up at last, realising that he was not doing the slightest good, and only wasting valuable energy.

His brain was growing clearer every minute, and he began to think over what had happened. Could Taverner, the ancient doorkeeper, be at the bottom of this? It seemed scarcely possible, and yet he must be. So far as White knew, nobody else was aware of his presence in Manchester. The man had told someone of his arrival and the line his enquiries were taking, and this trap had been set for him. In which case, Taverner was in it. It was only a natural sequence to suppose that he knew the mysterious Nottingham Deane and had warned him that someone was trying to trace him. Yet the old door-keeper had appeared genuine enough. Most likely he had been heavily bribed; that he was open to accepting one, the secretary had proved.

His thoughts broke off, and he listened intently as he heard the faint sound of shuffling footsteps, and presently caught sight of a crack of light that appeared underneath what must have been a door. The footsteps stopped, there came the click of a key, and a flood of light made him blink after the intense darkness.

Framed in the open doorway, illuminated by the light of the candle he carried, stood the figure of a man. He was dressed in a long black coat that reached almost to his heels, and where his face should have been was nothing but a white patch. In the flickering yellow flame of the candle, he looked weird and unreal. Peering through narrow slits in the white mask, he came forward, holding the light above his head.

'So you're awake, are you?' he muttered

in a low, hoarse whisper.

'I'm very much awake!' answered White angrily. 'What's the idea — '

'The idea is to stop you poking your nose into matters that don't concern you!' was the retort.

The masked man set the candle down on a narrow ledge over the small fireplace and, coming over, stood looking down at his captive menacingly.

'Who are you, and how long do you propose to keep me here?' demanded the secretary.

'Who I am is none of your business!' snarled the faceless man. 'As to how long you'll be kept here — well, it won't be very long, though when you leave you won't know much about it!'

There was a threat in the soft, whispering, obviously disguised voice, and Arnold felt a little coldness at his heart. There was no mistaking the man's meaning.

'Who sent you to make enquiries at the Grand?' continued the unknown.

'That's my business!' snapped White.

'Stubborn, eh? Well, it doesn't matter much. You haven't learnt much. You haven't learnt anything.'

'I've found what I came to find,' answered Arnold. 'I've found Nottingham Deane!'

The eyes through the slits in the mask glittered. 'If you think I'm Nottingham Deane,' said the man sharply, 'you're wrong. Nottingham Deane isn't in England.'

'Is that so? I'd bet he's not two yards away from me at the present moment.'

'You'd lose! Anyway, it doesn't matter. Whatever you've discovered, you'll never be able to use your knowledge. You've got about three hours more of life, my friend; make the most of it.' He took a handkerchief out of his pocket and, stooping quickly, tied it tightly about White's mouth. 'That's a precaution I forgot,' he murmured, straightening up after completing his task, 'but I didn't think you'd recover so quickly.' He went over and picked up the candle. 'You can rest for a little while now,' he said as he crossed to the door. 'I shall come back shortly.' He exited, closing and locking the door behind him; and once more Arnold was left in utter darkness.

His position was anything but a pleasant one. He had no idea what lay behind it all, but he was convinced that the man into whose hands he had fallen was the mysterious Nottingham Deane, and that the threat he had uttered was no idle one. His next visit would be the end of everything, so far as Arnold was concerned. There was only one thing to do, and that was to get out before he came, which was not the easiest thing in the world. Once more he made an endeavour to free his wrists, but with no more success than previously. The mysterious man had done a good job of tying the knots, for they were immovable.

He lay back, a little breathless from his exertions, and stared into the darkness, wracking his brains to try and discover a means of escape. If he was going to do anything, it had to be done quickly; there was very little time to waste.

During the period the man had been in the room, he had taken stock of his surroundings; and now he conjured up a mental picture, trying to recollect if there was anything that would suggest a means of freeing himself. It was a bare apartment, unfurnished, except for a broken chair and the pile of sacks on which he lay.

Facing him was a small window, heavily shuttered, and to his right the door through which the unknown had come. A tiny fireplace, devoid of fender or fireirons, completed he contents of the room. Nothing very inspiring among the collection. Certainly nothing that suggested a means of escape.

His heart sank. It seemed hopeless. And then he remembered one other object in the room which he had overlooked in his mental inventory. Beside the shuttered window projected a gas bracket, and attached to this he had noticed a dirty glass globe.

His spirits rose a little as an idea occurred to him. If in some way he could succeed in breaking that globe, there was the chance that he might be able to cut through the cords at his wrists with one of the sharp edges! It was a very slender hope, but it was worth trying.

His first problem was to get within reach of the globe. With difficulty, he rolled himself off the pile of sacks and began slowly and laboriously to wriggle in the direction of the gas bracket. The pitch darkness made his task harder, for he could see nothing, and had more or less to guess the position of his objective. It took him a long time, and he was breathless and sore when he was brought up with a bump against the wall. Fervently hoping that it was the right wall, he allowed himself to rest for a moment.

When he had recovered his breath, he set about the most difficult part of his task. With his hands tied behind his back and his legs bound at the ankles, it was by no means an easy feat to raise himself to an erect position, and that was what he was attempting to do; for, he concluded, if by the assistance of the wall he could manage to get on his feet, he would be able to break the glass of the globe with his head.

He started by sitting up with his back against the wall, and then, drawing up his legs, attempted to raise himself. It was difficult, however. Five times he failed and fell back. By the time he at last succeeded, he was a mass of aches from head to foot.

The next thing was to find the position of the gas bracket in that dense blackness. So far as he could judge, it ought to lie a foot or so to his right. Leaning against the wall, he shuffled sideways; and presently, to his delight, felt his head bump gently against the thing he sought. He could feel the globe, and after several attempts succeeded in snapping it from its flimsy support. It fell to the floor and he had the satisfaction of hearing it smash.

There followed another period of difficulty, for he had to lower himself again. This, however, was easier than getting up. When he was once more prone on the floor, he began to wriggle his way towards the spot where the broken glass lay. It took him a long time to get his fingers on a suitable piece, but at last he managed it; and after that it was a fairly simple task. His fingers were cut and bleeding, but he gave a sigh of relief when he felt the first strand of rope part beneath the keen edge; and a few minutes later his hands were free.

For a second or two, he lay still to ease his cramped fingers, and then started on the rope round his ankles. Five minutes later, he was able to stagger thankfully to his feet.

Searching his pockets, he discovered that none of his property had been taken; and finding matches, he struck one and made a tour of inspection. Beyond the pile of sacks on which he had been thrown, the room was empty. It was indescribably dirty and had obviously not been used for a very long time. He tried the door, but as he had expected, it was locked; and bending down, he could see the key. It was not a very substantial door, and he concluded that it would take very little effort to break it open; but the noise involved would without a doubt bring his captor immediately, and that was the last thing he wanted. The man was armed, and he himself was not; and if nothing worse happened, all chance of escape would be frustrated. He made an examination of the shuttered window and quickly discovered that without noise, this was as impassable as the door.

Frowning, he tried to evolve some means of getting out of that room. He was still vainly exercising his brains when he heard the faint sound of footsteps and realised that the masked man was returning.

Instantly a plan suggested itself. Tiptoeing across the room, he pressed himself against the wall near the door and waited, holding his breath. There was a fumbling at the key and the door swung open. A glimmer of light flickered across the threshold, and dimly he saw the figure of the man come in and peer in the direction of the place where he expected to see the helpless figure of his prisoner.

A gasp left his lips as he saw that the pile of sacking was empty, and then White acted. With a bound, he sprang onto the shoulders of the other, wrapping his arms and legs round him. He heard a strangled oath, and the candle the man was carrying flew from his hand and went out as they both crashed heavily to the floor.

With remarkable strength, the man wrenched himself free and tried to get to his feet, but Arnold's hand caught his ankle and brought him down again. With a snarl of rage, he turned; Arnold felt strong fingers clutch at his throat, and in spite of his efforts could not shake them off.

The strangling grip tightened, and with his head bursting he felt his resisting power ebb away. In a last desperate effort, he brought up his knee sharply, heard a grunt of pain, and the grip relaxed. Quickly following up his advantage, he flung his adversary off and staggered to his feet. He heard the other stumbling about in the dark and lashed out in the direction of the sound. His bunched fist met flesh, and then the man closed with him, fighting desperately.

They brought up with a crash against a wall. Arnold felt a foot twine round his ankle and then he fell heavily, striking his head on the floor. The impact dazed him. Before he could recover sufficiently to scramble to his feet, his opponent pulled open the door, and he heard his receding footsteps hurrying down the stairs. There came the thud of a door slamming; and then, as he ruefully picked himself up, the noise of a motor engine and the whine of a car as it was driven off.

The mysterious Mr. Nottingham Deane, if indeed it had been he, had succeeded in making his escape!

9

The Tragedy at Twenty-three

It was useless attempting to follow the man, and after resting for a moment or two to recover from the effects of his fall, Arnold struck a match and searched for the candle. He found it over by the fireplace, and lighting it began an examination of the house.

It was empty, and had apparently been so for a very long time. Hurriedly he went from room to room, discovering that each was as bare and desolate as the one in which he had been incarcerated. It struck him as being very queer. Where was the man he had come to meet? This was certainly not the lodging house he had expected to find. Nobody had lived here for years, judging by the state of the place. The paint was old and dirty, the paper peeling from the walls, the ceilings cracked; and there was dust everywhere.

But if Taverner had never lived here, then he must have been a party to the trap which had been set.

White was considerably puzzled. He would have staked his life on there being nothing criminal about Taverner. That grizzled man was the perfect type of doorkeeper, and it seemed ridiculous to connect him for a moment with Nottingham Deane. And yet Taverner must have been in it. He had made no mistake about the address, and it was Taverner who had given it to him. He must have known that the place was empty, and that the unknown man would be waiting for his arrival. Arnold's face set a little grimly. Unless Taverner had bolted, he was going to find himself in trouble.

He completed his search of the house, finding to his disappointment nothing that would help in tracing the man who had made him prisoner. In the dirty kitchen he had a wash at the sink, drying himself as best he could on his handkerchief, and generally tidied his dishevelled appearance.

It was beginning to get light. The faint

cold grey of early dawn filtered through the grimy windows. He realised for the first time that he was desperately hungry, and decided to make his way back to his hotel and have an early breakfast before going round to the Grand Cinema and tackling Mr. Taverner.

Opening the front door, he stepped out onto the pavement and glanced up at the knocker to assure himself that he had made no mistake. There it was, number twenty-three, the number the doorkeeper had given him at the theatre. That settled it. Taverner *had* been in the plot. And then, looking more closely, he discovered just how simply he had been tricked. The solution came to his mind like a flash. What a colossal fool he had been not to think of it before. But it was only now, in the morning light, that he was able to see how clean and new the brass figures were in comparison to the dirty paint on the door.

He moved along the pavement and looked at the house on the right hand side. It was also empty and bore the number twenty-five. He remembered glancing at it as he passed and seeing twenty-three on the next doorway had naturally taken it for granted that it was the one he was seeking. An inspection of the number on the other house next to the empty one confirmed his suspicion — it was twenty-nine!

The real number of the house to which he had come on the previous night was twenty-seven. The man who had set the trap for him had changed it. He could see now where the original number had been obliterated and the brass figures screwed on. The real twenty-three was further down the street.

This discovery, however, didn't absolve Taverner from complicity. It must have been through him that the masked man had become aware of the appointment, unless his conversation had been overheard. There was a possibility of that. He had taken no precaution to render his interview with Taverner secret, and anyone who had been lurking in the alleyway near the stage door could have heard the gist of their conversation. Perhaps that was it — perhaps his first impression of Taverner had been right, and the man had nothing to do with it.

He decided to change his plans. Instead of going back to his hotel, he would try and see Taverner at once, even if it meant knocking him up and risking his legitimate annoyance at being disturbed at that hour.

Walking slowly along the misty street, he came presently to the house he was seeking. The number was painted in dingy black, and blended so well with the nondescript hue of the door itself that it was almost undecipherable. Raising his hand, he gave a sharp tattoo on the knocker and waited. Nothing happened. After a little while he knocked again, with the same result; but it was not until his third and loudest assault on the door that he heard any sound in the silent house. Then there came to his ears the shuffling of slippered feet, followed by the rattle of a chain. The door was opened an inch or two, and the red sleepy face of a woman peered out at him.

'What d'you want?' demanded a voice husky with sleep. 'What d'you mean by knocking respectable people up at this hour?'

'I'm sorry,' said Arnold politely. 'Does Mr. Taverner live here?'

'Yes, 'e do!' retorted the woman ungraciously. 'But 'e's abed and asleep. What d'you want with him?'

'I'd like to see him for a few minutes.'

'He won't thank me for waking him,' said the woman crossly. 'Can't you come back later? This is a nice time, I must say, to come banging people up!'

'It's very urgent!' His tone was apologetic but firm.

'I suppose you'd better come in then,' grumbled the woman, and she opened the door wider.

He caught a glimpse of a faded flannel dressing-gown draped round the stout form of an elderly woman, whose grey hair hung over a florid face, as he stepped across the threshold.

'Mr. Taverner's room's at the top of the 'ouse,' she grunted as she closed the door. 'Who shall I say wants 'im?'

'Tell him it's the gentleman who interviewed him at the theatre last night,' said Arnold; and, leaving him in the narrow passage, the landlady began to ascend the staircase.

He heard her stop at the first landing and then continue on her way up the second flight. There was a pause, and then the thudding of her fist on the panel of a door came to his ears. After an interval the sound was repeated, followed by another period of silence. And then the stillness was broken suddenly by a scream that brought Arnold's heart to his mouth and sent him hurrying up the stairs two at a time.

He reached the small landing and called: 'What's the matter? What is it?'

There was no answer, and without waiting he mounted the second flight. Near the top of this, he saw the huddled figure of the landlady. She was lying motionless outside the open door of a room that gave onto a little passage. A glance showed him that she had fainted; and peering into the room on the threshold of which she lay, he saw the cause of her alarm.

It was a small apartment, furnished sparsely as a bedsitting room. Opposite

94

the door was a window, the curtains of which had not been drawn, and beneath this a bed; and it was the bed and its occupant that riveted his attention. Lying half in and half out of the disordered bed so that his head and shoulders almost touched the floor was the figure of the aged doorkeeper. The sheets were dappled red with blood, and from his thin bare chest protruded the handle of a knife! It only needed one look at the distorted face and staring eyes to see that he was dead.

But it was neither this fact, nor the manner of his death, that sent the breath hissing through White's clenched teeth. It was the sight of the little silver bell that had been pinned to the lapel of the faded pyjama jacket!

★   ★   ★

It was very late when Trevor Lowe got back to his flat after leaving Mr. Meek, and he had plenty to occupy his mind. The discovery of the missing volume from Mr. Bookham's collection had opened up a fresh avenue for investigation. With the assistance of the amazed draper, he had made an examination of the dead undertaker's house, and the method by which the unknown stealer of the book had effected an entrance was quickly discovered.

The catch of the kitchen window, a flimsy affair, had been forced back, and there were minute traces of earth beneath, proving definitely that this was the way the intruder had entered. He had, however, left no clue behind him which was likely to point to his identity. The rest of the house had not been touched, so it was evident that whoever had broken in had done so solely in order to acquire that volume of old press cuttings.

With Mr. Meek's help, Lowe was able to establish the fact that the stolen book had been the first of Mr. Bookham's collection, and had most likely contained an account of that sensational trial during which he had served on the jury. Was it this that held the clue to the whole business? The motive behind the series of mysterious murders that had baffled Scotland Yard? It seemed more than likely, otherwise the unknown person would never have gone to so much trouble and risk to acquire that volume of ancient newspaper cuttings. This twenty-four-year-old murder trial must form the genesis of these later crimes, and it should not be difficult to discover what the case was in which the dead undertaker had played such a prominent part.

10

The Missing Envelope

Before Arnold could enter that room of death, he heard the sound of excited voices below, and hurried footsteps ascending the stairs.

'Kate!' called the deep gruff tones of a man anxiously. 'What 'appened?'

An elderly man with ruffled grey hair came into view, obviously hastily aroused from sleep, and behind him Arnold caught a glimpse of a youth. They stared in open-mouthed astonishment as they saw him, and then the elder man noticed the prone figure of the woman and uttered a startled exclamation.

''Ere!' he began threateningly. 'What's been 'appening? What 'ave you done to my — '

'A serious crime has been committed,' interrupted the secretary sharply. 'There's nothing much the matter with your

98

wife — ' He guessed the relationship.
' — she's fainted, that's all, from shock.'

'A serious crime?' repeated the grey-haired man dazedly. 'What d'you mean? Who are you?'

'Never mind who I am!' snapped the secretary. 'Get your wife some water, that'll bring her round, and then one of you go for the police. Your lodger, Mr. Taverner, has been murdered!'

'Murdered?' It was the youth who breathed the ominous word, a weedy individual with a sallow pimply face. 'Blimey! Who done it?'

'That's for the police to find out,' said White impatiently. 'Don't waste time; go and see if you can find a policeman!'

They gaped at him stupidly, evidently unable to take in the meaning of this tragedy that had irrupted into the dull course of their lives; and Arnold was just going to repeat his order when a moan from the woman attracted their attention. She opened her eyes, gazed vaguely about her for a moment, and then struggled up on her elbow.

'My gawd, did you see 'im?' she

whispered. 'Lyin' there . . . all over blood . . . ' Her voice trailed away and she shuddered violently.

'It's all right, madam,' said Arnold soothingly. 'I've told your husband to go and notify the police.'

'What's it all about, Kate?' asked the elderly man, rubbing at his tousled hair. 'Is this true what 'e says — that Taverner's been done in?'

She nodded, her fearful eyes on the open doorway. 'Yes, 'e's been done in all right. You'd better do what this young feller says, an' fetch the police.'

'You go, Jim,' said the man, addressing the youth, who was staring in a fascinated way at the bedroom door. 'You go; I'll look after Mother.' He bent and assisted the woman to her feet, and she stood leaning against the wall, shaking, the red gone from her face.

'Can't I 'ave a look — ' began the youth, but his father swung round on him quickly.

'Do as you're told, will yer?' he cried. 'And look sharp about it!'

The youth muttered something below

his breath and hurried away down the stairs.

'Now,' said the grey-haired man when he had gone, 'let's see what this is all about.'

'I don't think you'd better go further than the doorway,' warned White as he advanced towards Taverner's room. 'No one ought to go in until after the police have been.'

'That's right,' chimed in the woman. 'Don't you go gettin' mixed up in it, George.'

'There's no 'arm in 'aving a look, is there?' grunted George, and he peered in. 'Struth!' he exclaimed a moment later. 'Who could 'a done this?'

'You didn't hear anything during the night?' asked Arnold.

'Nothing!' said the woman. 'We was sleepin' sound until your knockin' woke us up.'

'Poor old Taverner,' muttered her husband. 'Who'd 'ave thought anythin' like this would 'ave 'appened to 'im. Who'd want to croak 'im, anyway?'

Neither of them answered him because

neither of them knew. Arnold White had a pretty shrewd idea why the old doorkeeper had been killed, but he had no intention of putting it into words. In that first hasty glance round the bedsitting room, he had seen evidence of a thorough search. Drawers had been pulled open and their contents scattered about the floor, and he guessed that the reason for that search had been the envelope Nottingham Deane had dropped on the night he had visited Gloria Swayne at the old Grand Theatre, the envelope which Taverner had stated was still in his possession. He realised now that the doorkeeper had had nothing to do with the trap which had been set for him. His conversation with the old man had been overheard. That the masked man of the empty house was responsible for the murder of Taverner he was pretty sure, and it seemed reasonable to suppose that he was the same man who had passed under the name of Nottingham Deane; but this was only conjecture. He had no proof, although in his own mind he thought proof was scarcely necessary.

So far as he could see, the man who

called himself Nottingham Deane was the only person who could have benefited in any way by the doorkeeper's death. Taverner had been killed because he had in his possession evidence that might lead to the identity of that mysterious individual who, nearly five years before, had made Gloria Swayne sign that extraordinary contract.

'How do you come into this?' The suspicious voice of the grey-haired man broke in on his thoughts. 'What did you come to see old Taverner for?'

''E couldn't 'ave 'ad nothin' to do with it,' put in his wife. ''E was downstairs in the 'all when I found 'im.'

'I came to see Mr. Taverner on a matter of business,' said White. 'I saw him last night at the Grand Cinema.'

'Bit early to call on business, wasn't it?' George's voice was still full of suspicion. 'Funny time to talk business.'

'The matter was urgent,' explained Arnold shortly. He had no intention of going into details with these people, and fortunately at that moment the youth returned with a police constable whom he said he had providentially discovered at the end of the road.

The officer was a young man, and, to the secretary's relief, blessed with an intelligence above the average. He drew him aside and briefly explained what had happened, giving his name and address.

'I'll have to get in touch with the station,' said the constable when he had jotted down the particulars Arnold had given him. 'Will you see that nobody disturbs anything while I go and find a telephone?'

White agreed eagerly. He had been hoping for a chance to get a look round before the police began their investigations. The constable departed hurriedly, and when he had gone Arnold slipped into the room and closed the door.

He was careful not to touch anything that might yield a clue, contenting himself with a quick scrutiny which registered the appearance of the room on his mind. The dead man's personal possessions were meagre. An old cardboard box had been turned upside down on the table and its contents strewn over the dingy cloth. They consisted of old programmes, throwaways, aged photographs, and a miscellaneous collection of mementoes culled during the days when the Grand had been a theatre. Evidently amongst these was the most likely place for the old doorkeeper to have kept the envelope he had mentioned, but there was no sign of it. If it had been there, the murderer had found it and taken it away with him.

The method by which he had gained admittance to the house was simple. The bedroom window was open, and reared against the sill was a long ladder that led down to a small square back yard. An enquiry to the curious group on the landing elicited from Mr. Licket — that was the tenant's name — the fact that the ladder belonged to the people next door. A low wooden fence divided the yards from one another, and it would have been easy for the unknown to have climbed over from the empty house, set up the ladder, and carried out his dreadful work. It was more than likely that the murder had been committed during the interval between his first and second visit to White in the empty house.

The constable returned with the information that his superintendent was on his way with the police doctor. They arrived a few moments later, accompanied by a sergeant and another constable. The superintendent, a lean grey-haired man, listened to what Arnold White had to tell him while the doctor made his examination.

'The Yard will come into this, of course,' he said. 'The bell links it up with the other crimes, and they're bound to. You can give us no description of this man who coshed you at the empty house?'

White shook his head. 'Nothing that would be of any use,' he said.

The doctor interrupted them to make his report. The blow had been struck with considerable force, and the knife had severed one of the big vessels of the heart. Death had been practically instantaneous.

'I don't suppose he even had time to cry out,' he concluded. 'He must have died almost before he knew what had happened to him.' This accounted for the fact that the other tenants of the house had heard nothing.

At the superintendent's request, Arnold waited while the preliminary investigations were completed; and then, after answering a few more questions, he was allowed to go. Now that the excitement was over, he realised how tired he was. His eyes were hot, and there was a tightness about his temples and a dull ache in his head that was not entirely due to the effects of the blow he had received.

A taxi took him to his hotel; and when he had ordered breakfast, he made his way to the telephone and put through a call to London to acquaint Trevor Lowe with the tragic result of his visit to Manchester.

11

Trevor Lowe Gets Busy

The telephone call woke Lowe from a deep sleep. Before going to bed, he had, as was his usual practice, switched the instrument through to his room, and the shrill summons of the bell brought him back to consciousness. The call was very clear, and he listened while White briefly told him what had happened.

'What shall I do?' the secretary concluded.

'Come back to London by the first available train,' answered the dramatist. 'There's nothing you can do in Manchester.'

He hung up the receiver and, getting out of bed, pulled on his dressing gown. All further desire for sleep had left him, and making his way to the bathroom he shaved, had a cold bath, and dressing, went into his study.

He glanced through his mail, discovered with relief that there was nothing of importance, wrote to his agents concerning the film rights of his latest play, and when he had had breakfast put on his hat and coat and went out. A taxi carried him to Fleet Street, and set him down at the entrance to the big building which housed the activities of the *Post News*. Half an hour later he was immersed in the back files of that enterprising newspaper, searching diligently for that twenty-four year-old crime with which the dead undertaker had been connected — and suddenly he found it. From those ancient pages a name leapt at him; a name that brought him up with a jerk and a stifled exclamation!

With compressed lips and eager eyes, he read on; and in this account of a murder trial which in its day had been the sensation of the country, he found what he had been seeking. Here in these yellowing sheets was the beginning of the dreadful business that had culminated in the murder of Richard Sinclair, the death of the retired grocer at Midthorpe, the killing of the diamond merchant, and the murder of the undertaker. There was no doubt. The name of the principal person concerned formed an unmistakable link between this twenty-four-year-old crime and the token of the silver bell.

Lowe was thoughtful as he was driven back to his flat. Part of the mystery he had set out to solve was clear. He was still unaware of the identity of the person responsible for the bell murders; still unaware how Gloria Swayne came into it and the reason for that strange contract the mysterious Nottingham Deane had forced her to sign. But why the little silver token had been pinned to the coats of the murdered men was no longer a mystery. The motive for that was as transparent as glass.

As soon as he got back to his flat, he put through a call to the Manchester Branch of the London and Counties Bank and spoke to the manager, giving Shadgold's name and explaining what he wanted to know. After some hesitation and argument, the bank official gave him what information he had at his disposal. It wasn't much.

He remembered the account well. It had been an unusual one, and although it had since been transferred to one of the London branches, the circumstances surrounding it still remained clear in the manager's memory. The cheque for the initial deposit for fifty thousand pounds had come from a London firm of solicitors, Messrs. Crabbe, Dawson and Crabbe of Bedford Row, accompanied by a letter asking that an account should be opened with the proceeds of the cheque in the name of Miss Gloria Swayne. The solicitors had furnished the necessary references, and two days after, Miss Swayne had called and the formalities concerning the opening of the account were completed. The manager had never heard of Mr. Nottingham Deane, although he had a hazy recollection that Miss Swayne had mentioned the name. That was all the information he had to offer. It wasn't a great deal, but it suggested a fresh line of enquiry.

Lowe looked up the address of Messrs. Crabbe, Dawson and Crabbe and telephoned for an appointment. At twelve o'clock he was shown into the office of

Mr. Simon Crabbe, the senior member of the firm, an elderly thin-faced man who received him courteously.

'I've not had the pleasure of meeting you before, Mr. Lowe,' he greeted, 'but of course I know of you, and I've seen several of your plays. I confess I'm rather curious to learn why you've called to see me.'

'Your curiosity can easily be satisfied,' said the dramatist, dropping into the ancient leather chair which the lawyer indicated. 'I've called because I want you to give me some information concerning a client of yours.'

The lawyer's mouth tightened, and his eyes narrowed. 'It's not usual for solicitors to give information concerning their clients,' he said. 'You must know that, sir, as well as I do. What's the name of the particular client you refer to?'

'He calls himself Nottingham Deane,' answered Lowe, 'though whether that's his real name or not, you're probably in a better position to know than me.'

Mr. Crabbe's eyes opened wide. 'I know Mr. Deane,' he said. 'He is, or rather was,' he corrected himself hastily, 'a very good client of ours. I'm not altogether sure, however — '

'Mr. Crabbe,' broke in the dramatist, 'I appreciate your reticence, but I assure you I'm not asking out of idle curiosity. When I tell you I have a suspicion that your client, Mr. Deane, is mixed up in this series of crimes the newspapers have called the bell murders, you will, I feel sure, realise it's of vital importance that you should give me any help you can.'

His words startled the lawyer out of his habitual calm. 'Good gracious! You surely don't mean that, Mr. Lowe?' he exclaimed.

'I do,' replied Lowe, and he explained how he came to be connected with the affair.

There was a short interval of silence while Mr. Crabbe caressed his long chin thoughtfully. 'If you can assure me,' he said at last, 'that what you say is true, I'll endeavour to help you in every way I can. It's my duty to do so.'

'I *can* assure you,' said the dramatist, 'that even if Nottingham Deane isn't responsible for these murders directly, he's at least very closely connected with them.'

'What do you want to know about him?'

'Everything you can tell me.'

Crabbe smiled wryly. 'I'm afraid that's very little. The curious thing about Mr. Deane is that although we acted for him for a very long time, some four or five years, we never saw him.'

Lowe raised his eyebrows. 'That seems very odd,' he remarked.

'Let me qualify that statement,' replied the lawyer hastily. 'When I say we never saw him, I mean this: I *did* meet Mr. Nottingham Deane on several occasions, but, strange as it may appear to you, I have no idea what he was like.'

'Do you mean you never saw his face?' asked Lowe incredulously.

The lawyer nodded. 'I mean exactly that. His face had been so disfigured in a motor accident that he told me he habitually wore a white mask. As a consequence of this, our interviews with him took place at his own house, usually in a semi-dark room, as he was very sensitive about his appearance.'

Lowe pursed his lips. 'An excellent excuse to avoid recognition.'

'Possibly,' agreed Mr. Crabbe, 'but you'll realise that it wasn't our business to enquire too deeply into his reasons. If he wished to conduct his business in that way, it was really nothing to do with us.'

'I quite see that. So you wouldn't recognise him again if you saw him?'

'Quite frankly, I wouldn't. I know that he was stoutish and of medium height, but that's about all.'

'What was the nature of your dealings with him?' asked the dramatist.

Mr. Crabbe hesitated. The tradition of secrecy was obviously very firmly implanted in his system. 'Well,' he said at length, slowly, 'they were mostly of a confidential nature — he's a very wealthy man, and we have charge of a great number of investments; at least we had. As I told you, we're no longer acting for Mr. Deane. He took his business out of our hands a year ago.'

'Can you tell me the business he was interested in?'

'Mostly in films. He was the principal shareholder in a number of British companies.'

This was interesting, thought Lowe, for it cleared up one small point in Gloria Swayne's story that had troubled him. He had wondered how the mysterious Nottingham Deane had been so sure when he made his offer that she should play the leading part in *Women of the Dust*. Obviously, if he had been financially interested in the company which produced that film, it was easy.

'Was one of your commissions to trace a woman named Swayne?' he asked.

'Yes, that's right,' said Mr. Crabbe. 'We eventually found her playing in a theatre in Manchester — the Grand, I think it was.'

'And I presume it was your firm who drew up that extraordinary contract?'

An expression of surprise crossed the lawyer's face. 'So you know about that?' he murmured. 'Yes, we were responsible for that.'

'What was the motive behind it?' asked Lowe bluntly.

'I haven't the least idea,' Mr. Crabbe said, shaking his head. 'You'll understand, Mr. Lowe, it wasn't our business to reason why. We merely followed instructions; and if a man wants to give large sums of money away, that's his own affair.'

'I quite understand that,' murmured the dramatist.

'Once we traced her,' the lawyer went on, 'and she agreed to do what was required of her, then all that remained was for us to pay the money into the bank.' He looked at his visitor curiously. 'May I enquire how you knew about this contract?'

After a moment's consideration, Lowe told him of his interview with Gloria Swayne, and the lawyer listened interestedly.

'It was most peculiar, most peculiar!' he declared. 'I must confess I was very curious at the time to know what lay behind it, and I've often wondered since.'

'You were present at the interview that night after the theatre?' asked the dramatist.

'I was there with my managing clerk,' answered Mr. Crabbe. 'At Mr. Deane's request, we called ourselves Mr. Smith and Mr. Jones, if I remember rightly. I'm sure Miss Swayne thought we were all a little mad. That was the only occasion on which we've seen Mr. Deane without his mask, but throughout the interview he kept his face covered by a silk scarf, so it really made very little difference.'

'Then you've no idea,' persisted Lowe, 'why he desired this extraordinary contract made with Miss Swayne?'

'No idea at all!' declared the lawyer. 'That night was the last time we saw Mr. Deane; he disappeared completely after that. We had instructions to administer certain monies and to look after his not inconsiderable investments; and then a year ago he wrote from Los Angeles instructing us to transfer what money remained at his bank to another account, an account belonging to a man called Grandsire, which we did.'

'Grandsire?' repeated Lowe, and there was amazement in his voice. 'Isn't that the man who runs a mission in the East End?'

'It's more than likely,' said the lawyer,

'though I couldn't tell you for certain. I've never heard of the gentleman. The account, however, is at a bank in Stepney, so you're probably right.'

'Was the sum involved a large one?'

'Very large. There was nearly sixty thousand pounds in the current account, and over two hundred and forty thousand on deposit.'

'And was this huge amount transferred to Mr. Grandsire's account?'

The lawyer nodded. 'Every penny of it. And Mr. Deane's account, according to instructions, closed. We wrote to Los Angeles notifying him that we'd carried out his wishes, and received in reply a letter thanking us for all the trouble we'd been put to on his behalf and informing us that since he was not returning to England, he would no longer require our services. That, as I said, was just over a year ago, and from that time to this we've heard nothing further at all from Mr. Deane.'

'His behaviour, to say the least of it,' remarked Lowe, 'seems extremely eccentric. Where was the house in which this agreement with Miss Swayne was signed?'

'A place called Garston Manor, near the village of Garston, and about eleven miles from Manchester, on the London Road. It belonged to Mr. Deane.'

'Does it still belong to him?'

'So far as I know.'

Lowe rose to his feet. 'Then I think that's all, at least for the present,' he said pleasantly. 'I'm very grateful to you for your assistance, and I assure you that unless it has to be used in evidence, anything you've told me will be treated confidentially.'

'I'm glad to have been of help, Mr. Lowe,' said the lawyer as he shook hands, 'though I haven't been able to tell you much.'

'I think you've told me enough,' said Lowe, and he took his leave.

On the way back to Portland Place, he was a very thoughtful man. There was a lot to be done yet, but he was convinced that he had in his hands two of the threads that would lead him to the truth concerning the bell murders. One of these he discovered in that twenty-four-year-old account of a murder trial he had read that morning, and the other Mr. Crabbe had unconsciously given him when he mentioned the name of the man to whom Nottingham Deane had transferred all his money. A man did not pay such a large sum as three hundred thousand pounds into another's account without a very good reason, and so far as Lowe was concerned, the reason was obvious.

Mr. Grandsire of Stepney and Mr. Nottingham Deane of Garston Manor were one and the same!

12

Eight Doomed Men

Trevor Lowe elected to walk from the lawyer's office to his flat, and he was so occupied with what he had just learnt that it was not until he was halfway home that he remembered a visit he had planned to make. Stopping, he hailed a passing taxi and was driven to the Old Bailey, were he spent a considerable time.

He reached Portland Place to find Shadgold waiting in the study. The burly inspector looked tired and worried, and greeted the dramatist with an expression of relief.

'Glad you've got back, Mr. Lowe,' he said. 'I shouldn't have been able to wait much longer. There's been another of 'em, in Manchester this time.'

'I know,' said Lowe, crossing to the desk and filling his pipe. 'A man called Taverner was murdered at Twenty-three

Hulme Road in the early hours of this morning.'

The inspector's rather prominent eyes opened wide in astonishment. 'Now how the dickens did you know that?' he gasped. 'It wasn't in the morning papers.'

'No, it was White who told me. He was on the telephone first thing this morning.'

'On the telephone? Where from?' demanded the bewildered Shadgold.

'From Manchester,' said Lowe quietly. 'I sent him up to interview the dead man yesterday.'

Momentarily bereft of speech, Shadgold stared at him, rubbing at his short close-cropped hair. 'D'you mean to tell me, Mr. Lowe,' he said at last, 'that you knew this man was going to be killed?'

Lowe shook his head again and smiled. 'I had no idea he was going to be killed. White went up, as a matter of fact, to try and extract some information from him. If you'll stop striding up and down like a caged lion, I'll explain.'

The inspector dropped into a chair, which gave a protesting squeak under his weight; and when he had lit his pipe,

Lowe proceeded to tell him about Gloria Swayne's visit and the strange story she had related. Shadgold listened without comment, his florid face expressive of his astonishment.

'Do you think there's any truth in her idea?' he asked when the dramatist had finished. 'It seems a bit far-fetched to me.'

'I don't think there's the least truth in it!' declared Lowe. 'I think she's worrying herself unnecessarily. I'm practically certain that her acquaintance with these men who were killed was nothing more than a coincidence.'

'Hm! Peculiar coincidence, though. This last feller — Taverner — he knew her, too.'

'Yes, he knew her, too. But I'm of the opinion that the reason for his death wasn't the same reason as the others. I think he was killed because the murderer was under the impression that he knew too much; because he had in his possession that envelope.'

Shadgold gently rubbed at his nose. 'Which means the man we want is this fellow Nottingham Deane,' he said.

'It would appear so,' said the dramatist, but there was something in his tone that caused the inspector to look at him quickly.

'You don't seem too certain of it,' he remarked suspiciously.

'It's impossible to be certain of anything,' said Lowe with a slight smile; but Shadgold was not satisfied.

'It seems to me, Mr. Lowe,' he continued, 'that you know a lot more about this business than you've told me.'

Trevor Lowe blew a stream of smoke towards the ceiling and watched it slowly disperse before he replied. 'You're wrong and you're right, Shadgold. So far as actual facts are concerned, I know very little more than you do. But I have a theory I'm working on which I think may prove right.'

The Scotland Yard man sat up alertly. 'What is it?' he remarked, but Lowe shook his head.

'I'd rather not go into it at the moment. It might prove nothing more than a wild goose chase, in which event it's far better that I should keep it to myself. If I'm right, however, I think we can prevent any more murders.' Taking a little book from his pocket, he rapidly scribbled for a few moments on a sheet of paper. 'There,' he said, handing it to the inspector, 'are the names of eight people who in my opinion are in danger of being the next victims of the killer.'

Shadgold took the paper, and his expression of amazement was almost ludicrous. 'How in the world do you know?' he cried. 'How can you say who this lunatic has decided to kill next?'

'I can't. I never said I knew. I don't at the moment. All I'm prepared to say is that I *believe* the eight men whose names I've written there are in danger. I may be entirely wrong; but I think, as a matter of precaution, you should find out the present whereabouts of these people and have them watched.'

The bewildered inspector tugged angrily at his small moustache. 'I suppose it's useless asking you to be more explicit, Mr. Lowe.'

'Quite useless at the present. As I told you, I'm only working on a theory. When

I'm in a position to prove it, I'll tell you everything; but until then, I'd rather keep it to myself.'

'As usual,' murmured Shadgold. 'Though why in the world you can't let me in on it, I'm hanged if I know!'

Lowe smiled. 'For the reason that I've no desire to set you off on what may possibly be a false trail. If I'm wrong, well, there's no particular harm done; but there's no earthly reason why two of us should waste our time.'

Shadgold pinched a fold of loose skin below his chin savagely. This characteristic reticence on the part of the dramatist always annoyed him, and yet he knew from experience that it was useless arguing. Until Lowe had got the whole thing cut and dried, he would keep silent.

'Well, have it your own way, Mr. Lowe,' he said with a sigh. 'But don't keep me in the dark longer than you can help.'

'I'll promise you that.'

'In the meanwhile, I'll have these fellows traced up and put a man on to guard them. If you're right, and this crazy killer starts anything, he'll get a shock.'

'He's by no means crazy,' murmured the dramatist. 'At least, not in the accepted sense of the word. There's nothing haphazard about these crimes, Shadgold; there's method behind them. The man's got a kink, of course, but he's not just an ordinary homicidal maniac.'

'He'll make me one before he's done,' growled the inspector savagely, 'for it's getting unbearable at the Yard, Mr. Lowe. The Home Office is up on its hind legs, and the commissioner is being deluged with a series of curt notes demanding why the police haven't succeeded in apprehending this fellow. Naturally he's not feeling very happy about it, and he vents his feelings on me. I'm hauled up on the carpet on an average twice a day to report how the investigation's proceeding.'

'Well, you'll be able to tell him that you're taking steps to prevent any further crimes.'

'That'll certainly be something,' admitted Shadgold grudgingly, and he looked at his watch. 'Now I must go. I've got to go up to Manchester and look into this new murder.'

'Do you know anything about a man called Grandsire?' asked Lowe as he was turning towards the door.

Shadgold looked round sharply. 'That's the man who runs a place called the Providence Mission at Stepney,' he answered. 'Why are you interested in him?'

'Because I think he may be intimately connected with this business.'

'Do you mean you think he's the fellow we're after?'

'I wouldn't go so far as to say that,' said Lowe cautiously, 'but I believe he knows quite a lot about it. What sort of man is he?'

The Scotland Yard man told him all that was known concerning Mr. Grandsire, and he listened interestedly.

'Hm!' he commented. 'He seems quite a mysterious individual.'

'We've always regarded him as harmless,' replied Shadgold. 'Rather an eccentric old gentleman, but that's all. At one time I believe there was a suspicion that he was a fence, but nothing could ever be proved. How does he come into this business?'

'He may *not* come into it,' said Lowe

evasively. 'It's only an idea of mine.'

Shadgold looked at him steadily. 'I know these ideas of yours of old, Mr. Lowe,' he retorted. 'What d'you want me to do about Grandsire?'

'Nothing,' said Lowe hastily. 'I don't want you to do anything, Shadgold. I'll attend to Grandsire myself.'

'All right,' said the inspector resignedly. 'I suppose you'll work your own way. I must get off now,' he added. 'I'll be back late tonight, or first thing in the morning if you want me.'

He had barely taken his departure when the housekeeper appeared and informed Lowe that lunch was ready. 'An' if it's spoiled and not fit for human consumption, it's not my fault,' she grumbled. 'I've had it ready and waiting this past hour and more.'

'I'm sure it will be excellent,' said Lowe, cutting short her protestations, and he followed her into the dining-room.

When he had finished his meal, he came back to the study and considered his next move. There was so much to be done that he could not quite decide where to begin. It was essential that as soon as possible, contact should be made with Mr. Grandsire, whom he more than suspected of being the mysterious Nottingham Deane; but any investigation in this direction would have to be carried out warily. The man's suspicions must on no account be aroused.

Over a thoughtful pipe, he consulted the notes he had made earlier that morning and the list of names, a copy of which he had given Shadgold. After twenty minutes he came to a decision, and scribbling a note, he left it on the desk for White and went out.

A cab took him to Tooley Street and set him down in the middle of that narrow thoroughfare in front of an old block of offices. He paid the cabman and passed into the dark entrance, unaware that the line of enquiry he was following was to kill two birds with one stone, and eventually lead him to make the acquaintance of Mr. Grandsire, whose other name he believed to be Nottingham Deane.

The offices of Messrs. Freeman and

Samuels occupied the third floor, as a dingy inscription and the whitewashed wall testified; and mounting the stairs, he pushed open a dirty glass door marked 'General Office'. Immediately inside the door was a stained counter on which stood a rusty bell. He pressed it. A sleepy-eyed boy poked his head round a screen in answer to its summons.

'Yes, sir?' he enquired languidly.

'Could you tell me if you have a Mr. Simmons working here?' asked the dramatist.

The boy screwed up his face and shook his head. 'Not in my time. But I ain't been 'ere very long. I'll ask.'

He disappeared into an inner office, and presently returned, followed by a gloomy-looking man with a bald head and a large expanse of moustache. 'Were you enquiring for Mr. Simmons, sir?' asked this individual.

Lowe nodded.

'He's left here now,' said the man. 'He left about two years ago when we had a reorganisation.'

'That's very annoying,' said Lowe.

'Have you any idea where I can find him?'

'He got a job with the Billeter Trading Company, Sixteen Fenchurch Street, I believe.'

'Thank you.' Lowe made a note of the address. 'I'm very much obliged to you.'

'Not at all.' The other waved away his thanks with a not very clean hand. 'I should be glad if you'd remember me to him, if you see him. The name is Glober.'

'I will,' promised Lowe, and he hurried down the stairs.

Enquiries at the Billeter Trading Company, however, proved disappointing. Mr. Simmons had worked for them, but he had left six months previously. They were able to supply Lowe with the address at which he lived while he had been in their employment, One hundred and eleven Cable Buildings, Stepney.

Stepney! It crossed the dramatist's mind that this was where the Providence Mission was situated.

He thanked his informant, and leaving the offices of the Billeter Trading Company, made his way by Tube to Stepney. Coming out of the station, he enquired his way to Cable Buildings.

'Third left, fourth right, you can't miss it,' said the man he had asked.

He found the place without difficulty, a narrow cul-de-sac lined on either side with disreputable tenement houses. Number one hundred and eleven, he found, was on the top floor of a building at the end of the street, and, a little breathless from climbing the stairs, he knocked. The door was opened by a faded woman of uncertain age.

'Does Mr. Simmons live here?' he enquired.

The woman shook her head. ''E's gone,' she answered. 'Been gone for more than a month. Sneaked off in the night, 'e did, owin' me three weeks' rent. What are you after 'im for, mister?'

'I have some information to give him,' answered Lowe evasively. 'Have you any idea where he can be found?'

'You might find 'im at the Prov.'

'Prov?' he repeated.

'The Providence Mission;' she snapped curtly. 'They takes in people what's down on their luck.'

'Oh, yes, I've heard of it,' said the dramatist; and he was struck by the extraordinary coincidence that had led this man he was seeking to Mr. Grandsire's home for the destitute. 'Is that very far from here?'

She directed him ungraciously, and he descended the worn stone stairs to the street once more. The mission was only ten minutes' walk away, and presently he found himself at the door of the ugly building. Cosh Willis answered his knock, and eyed him suspiciously when he made his enquiry.

'Yus, we've got a bloke called Simmons 'ere,' he said. 'Wot d'you want with 'im?'

'That's a private matter,' said Lowe, producing a pound note. 'Could I have a word with him?'

'I suppose you could,' said Mr. Willis, eyeing the note greedily, 'though we don't allow visitors as a rule.' He invited the dramatist into the plainly furnished airy hall, and closed the door. 'Come this way,' he said. 'Simmons was feelin' a bit groggy today, an' 'e's in bed.' He led the way up the stairs and down a long corridor. Opening a door at the end, he ushered Lowe into a narrow room that was furnished like a dormitory, with six beds running down on either side. 'That's 'im there,' he said, pointing to a bed at the far end.

Followed by the dramatist, he walked over to where the recumbent man lay, and, taking him by the shoulder, shook him gently. 'Wake up, chum,' he said. ''Ere's a bloke wants to see yer.'

There was no immediate answer, and Mr. Willis shook the man again. ''E ain't 'alf in a deep sleep,' he muttered; and then with an exclamation, Lowe pushed him aside and bent over the bed.

Mr. Simmons was indeed in a deep sleep — so deep that he would never again wake. The pillow under his head was red with the blood that oozed from the wound in his throat . . .

Gently the dramatist turned down the blankets that covered him. What he had expected to see was there — a tiny bell of silvery metal, pinned to the front of the dead man's torn and ragged shirt!

13

The Perturbation of Mr. Grandsire

'Blimey!' breathed Mr. Willis, his face white and his eyes staring.

Lowe swung quickly towards him. 'Fetch the proprietor of this place,' he said sternly, 'and telephone the police.'

'The guv'nor ain't in,' said Cosh. ''E went out with a feller what called to see 'im about an hour ago.'

'Well, then, telephone the police!' snapped the dramatist. 'Go on, man. Don't stand staring there — this is serious!'

'I should blinking well say it is!' muttered Cosh. 'You wouldn't 'ave thought anyone would 'ave wanted to rub out a bloke like that — '

'Well, somebody did,' said Lowe curtly. 'And the longer you stand there talking, the better chance that somebody has of getting away. Go and do as I ask you.'

Mr. Willis obeyed without further argument, and, left to himself, the dramatist made a hasty examination of the room in which the crime had been committed. It was a long, narrow apartment with a window at one end. It was near this window that the bed on which the dead man lay was placed. The lower sash was raised a foot, and Lowe made an inspection of the linoleum-covered floor below, but there were no traces on the polished surface. Carefully he pushed the window fully up and leant out.

It faced onto a small backyard, and opposite it was the blank wall of some kind of factory. A few inches to one side was a narrow iron ladder screwed into the brickwork, evidently a rather primitive sort of fire escape. There were no marks on the thin film of soot that covered the sill, but it would have been possible for anyone to enter that way without leaving any. The lower part of the window came to within eighteen inches of the floor, and it would not have been difficult for an active man to have stepped directly from the iron ladder into the room.

The dramatist made a mental note of these facts, and turned his attention to the bed and the dead man. He lay on his side with his back to the window in the easy, natural position of a sleeper, and except for the horrid gash below the chin exhibited no signs of violence. Lowe concluded from this that he must have been asleep when death had come to him. The weapon had severed the jugular, and the bed was soaked with blood. The crimes had been committed swiftly and surely, and the murderer had left behind no clue.

He straightened up and looked down at all that remained of the unfortunate Mr. Simmons. One of the eight men whom he had warned Shadgold were in danger could be crossed off the list, and his death offered confirmation of Lowe's theory, for the out-of-work Mr. Simmons lad, together with Richard Sinclair, George Stone, Solomon Riess and Mr. Bookham the undertaker, formed part of the jury who, twenty-four years ago, had brought in a verdict of 'Guilty' against a woman for the murder of her husband.

There could be little doubt now concerning the motive behind this series of crimes. The question that remained to be answered was, who was responsible?

His search that morning among the records at the Old Bailey had disclosed the names of the twelve men who had sat on that jury. He had guessed that they were all in danger, but he had not expected that the danger would overtake Simmons so quickly. It had been purely chance that had made him select this man out of the eight to endeavour to trace, for it had occurred to him, after Shadgold had left, that an interview with one of the people who could possibly give him first-hand information concerning the trail would prove useful. There was a point he wanted to clear up, a point the man who lay motionless in front of him could have settled; and now he would have to seek that information elsewhere, perhaps from one of the remaining seven, if they could be located before the unknown silenced them forever.

Cosh Willis came back, his face still

showing traces of the shock he had sustained. 'I've been on the phone,' he announced, 'and the super's hopping along at the double.'

'Did you tell him what had happened?' asked Lowe.

The ex-convict nodded. 'Course I did. What d'you take me for? Blimey, this ain't half going to give the boss a turn!'

'You mean Mr. Grandsire?' asked the dramatist.

'Who else should I mean? Course I mean 'im.'

'When do you expect him back?'

'I dunno. Maybe an hour, maybe two.'

'You say he went out with a friend an hour ago?'

'That's right. A feller called to see 'im early this afternoon. 'E was shut up in the office talking for hours, and then the guv'nor and the bloke went out together.'

'Who was this man?'

'I never seen 'im before. Maybe 'e was a friend of the gov'nor's, maybe 'e wasn't. All sorts of people comes 'ere to see 'im, mostly trying to screw some dough out of 'im.' Cosh eyed his questioner narrowly.

'Are you a busy?' he enquired.

'Not exactly,' answered Lowe with a smile.

'Thought you was by the way you was firin' questions. What did you want with Simmons?' He jerked his head towards the bed.

'I just wanted to have a word with him. Did anybody else call this afternoon?'

Mr. Willis shook his head. 'Not a blinking soul!' he said. 'If they 'ad, I'd 'ave seen 'em, I was down in the 'all from two o'clock onwards.'

A sharp rat-tat on the knocker prohibited any further questions Lowe might have put, and a few seconds later the Providence Mission was in the hands of the police.

Lowe had met Superintendent Jameson once with Shadgold, and that thin-faced grey-haired man greeted him with surprise.

'What are you doing here, sir?' he said. 'Do you know anything about this business?'

The dramatist told him how he had come to make the discovery while the

142

divisional surgeon who had luckily been in the police station when Cosh had telephoned the news was making his examination.

'Hm!' commented the police official when Lowe had finished. 'So it was you and this fellow Willis who made the discovery, eh? It's been a surprise to me that nothing like this has ever happened here before. Old Grandsire's an eccentric old man, and the kind of people he harbours are — well . . . ' He shrugged his shoulders. 'I wouldn't put anything past them.'

'The man who did this killing,' said Lowe, 'is the same person who perpetrated the other murders, don't forget that. He's not just an ordinary crook.'

'They get crooks of all sorts here,' grunted the superintendent. 'It wouldn't surprise me to learn that there was a homicidal maniac among them. This fellow, Cosh Willis, is supposed to be reformed, but he's got one of the worst records you'd find in a day's march.'

'I'm convinced he didn't have anything to do with this crime,' replied Lowe. 'He was genuinely shocked when he saw the body.'

The doctor interrupted them to make his report. It was brief. Death had been caused by severing the jugular vein with some sharp instrument — the doctor suggested a razor, but was not prepared to swear to this — and the man had died almost instantaneously.

Jameson sent for Cosh Willis, and that 'reformed' character came uneasily.

'Now then, what do you know about this?' said the superintendent.

Mr. Willis's face assumed an expression of injured innocence. 'Me! What should I know about it? I don't know nothing. I'm a reformed character, I am!'

'I'll bet you are,' muttered the sceptical police official.

'You coulda knocked me down with a flat iron,' declared Cosh, 'when me and this feller found 'im.'

'How long has the man been living at this place?'

'H'off and h'on about three weeks. Nice quiet sort of bloke, 'e were, but there ain't much I can tell you about 'im.

As a rule, this 'ere place is only for them wot's got relatives inside, but this feller seemed such a sad case that the guv'nor allowed 'im to stay until 'e got a job. 'E used to come every evening about six, 'ave 'is meal, and then go up to bed. Always seemed to be tired like, and slept like a top until 'e was called with the rest at seven o'clock in the morning.'

'Today I understand he wasn't feeling very well,' said Jameson.

'That's right. When 'e was called this mornin', 'e complained of pains in 'is stomich and dizziness. I reported it to the guv'nor, and 'e told me to tell 'im to stay in bed. I took 'im up some tea and toast about one o'clock, and I didn't see 'im again until we found 'im. Blimey, it give me a turn, I can tell yer!'

'I expect it did,' said the superintendent, not at all interested in Mr. Willis's sensations. 'Who was in the mission during the afternoon?'

There had been nobody in, explained Mr. Willis, except himself, Mr. Grandsire, and the man who called to see him. The rest of the inmates were all out, either looking for work or loafing, he couldn't say which; but his tone implied what he thought. Several more questions were put to him, but he could supply no other information. He had spent most of the afternoon in the little porter's office that opened off the hall, and he had heard nothing.

Jameson grunted disappointedly. 'Unless Willis is lying,' he said when Cosh had been dismissed, 'it looks as though the murderer must have come from outside.'

Lowe could have offered another suggestion, but he wisely remained silent.

With his sergeant and one of the constables, the superintendent made an inspection of the premises, but found nothing to reward his search. An examination of the yard showed that it would have been quite easy for anyone to have gained admittance from the street. A narrow alleyway led down beside the Mission building, and a gate in the wall that surrounded the yard opened into this. The gate was locked, but it was not very high, and to an energetic man would have offered little or no obstacle.

They had returned to the long dormitory, where Jameson's men had just finished taking the usual police photographs and the superintendent was discussing the removal of the body, when there was a sudden commotion in the doorway.

'What are all these men doing here?' demanded an angry voice in the passage. 'Willis, where are you? You know I don't allow visitors! You should know better than to permit these men to come in here!'

'I couldn't help it, guv'nor,' answered the whining voice of Mr. Willis. 'There's — '

'Couldn't help it? Nonsense!' snapped Mr. Grandsire as he strode indignantly into the room, followed by the doorkeeper. 'Who are they? What do they want?'

Lowe turned and went forward to meet the speaker. 'I take it you're Mr. Grandsire?' he enquired.

The old man looked at him angrily. 'That's my name,' he replied. 'And who are you, may I ask?'

'My name is Trevor Lowe,' answered the dramatist, and Cosh Willis uttered an exclamation.

'Blimey!' he gasped. 'As near a busy as

dammit!' Lowe's connection with the police had become well known since the newspaper prominence given to the many cases in which he had assisted Inspector Shadgold.

'I regret to inform you, Mr. Grandsire,' put in Superintendent Jameson, coming forward, 'that a serious crime has been committed here. A man called Simmons has been murdered, and — '

'Murdered!' The grey-haired man's voice was horrified. 'Here? What do you mean? What are you talking about?'

For answer, Jameson pointed to the still form lying on the bed. Mr. Grandsire took a step forward and peered down, his face suddenly old and grey.

'Horrible!' he muttered. 'Horrible!' He shivered, and Lowe laid a hand on his arm. The old man looked round with a dazed expression in his eyes. 'It seems I owe you all an apology,' he muttered. 'For the moment I thought you were a band of curious sightseers. Have you any idea how — how this dreadful thing happened?'

The dramatist shook his head. 'At the moment, none, except that it's undoubtedly the work of the man commonly known as the silver bell murderer.'

'No, no, it can't be! It's impossible!' exclaimed Mr. Grandsire agitatedly. 'Impossible, I tell you!'

'Impossible or not it's a fact!' retorted Lowe.

'But why should he pick on a man like Simmons? There doesn't seem to be any reason — '

'There never is any reason at the time, Mr. Grandsire,' put in Jameson. 'It's only the light of investigation that lays bare the reason for any murder. I'm afraid you'll have to reconcile yourself to a certain amount of publicity.'

The other gave a resigned gesture. 'I can't prevent it, I suppose,' he said helplessly. 'It's a terrible thing! A terrible thing!' He shook his head. 'Have you discovered anything — any clue?' He looked at Jameson enquiringly.

'At present, no, sir,' replied the superintendent, and he turned away.

'Mr. Grandsire,' put in Lowe quickly, 'I should like to have a word or two with you in private.'

The old man looked at him, and the

dramatist could have sworn that there was a hint of fear in his eyes.

'Certainly, if you wish it,' he said after an almost imperceptible pause. 'Come to my office.'

He led the way downstairs to the ground floor and ushered his visitor into the comfortable apartment. 'Sit down, Mr. Lowe,' he said, taking his customary seat behind the desk and leaning wearily back in his chair. 'Now, what was your object in wishing to see me privately?'

Lowe settled himself in the chair and crossed his legs. 'Because, Mr. Grandsire,' he said smoothly, his eyes fixed on the other's face, 'I'm anxious to trace a man calling himself Nottingham Deane, and I think you can help me.'

The old man started as if he had been shot, and his already pale face went a ghastly grey.

'Nottingham Deane?' he mumbled. 'Nottingham Deane? I know nothing about Nottingham Deane.'

He gave a queer, strangled gasp and fell forward over the blotting pad.

14

The Mysterious Visitor

With an exclamation of alarm, Trevor Lowe sprang to his feet and bent over the motionless form of the old man. He was breathing stertorously and irregularly, and a flush of red had come into his face. The mention of Nottingham Deane had evidently given him a shock, which was understandable if he was that mysterious individual, as the dramatist believed.

A quick examination convinced him that it was nothing more serious than a fainting fit, and searching the apartment, he found a bell and pressed it. After a slight delay, Cosh Willis appeared at the door.

'Blimey!' exclaimed that startled man as his eyes caught sight of the slumped figure of his employer. 'What's 'appened?'

'Your master's fainted,' said Lowe curtly. 'And if there's any brandy in the place, you'd better bring some — and some water.'

'There's some brandy in the medicine cupboard in 'is bedroom,' volunteered Cosh, 'but I can't get at it; it's locked, and 'e keeps the key. You can't leave brandy where it's get-at-able in a place like this.'

Without replying, the dramatist lifted the limp form and, supporting it on one arm, searched the pockets of the old-fashioned Norfolk suit that Mr. Grandsire was wearing. He found a bunch of keys and tossed them over to the anxious doorkeeper.

'Here you are,' he said. 'Fetch the brandy, and don't drink any on the way.'

With an indignant protest at this suggested slur upon his honesty, Mr. Willis hurriedly departed. While he was gone, Lowe loosened the unconscious man's collar and opened the window. He was more than ever certain that this old man before him held the secret of Nottingham Deane, and that if he could be persuaded to speak, a great deal that was now obscure would be made clear.

Cosh Willis returned with a bottle of brandy under one arm and carrying a glass and a jug of water. ''Ere you are,' he said, putting them down on the desk. 'Anything else?'

'Yes; you can clear out. And leave those keys.'

'Look here,' said Mr. Willis belligerently, 'I ain't going to be ordered about by you. I've got somethin' to say — '

'Say it on the other side of the door,' broke in the dramatist, and taking the ex-convict by the arm, pushed him out of the office and shut the door behind him.

Coming back to the desk, he set about restoring Mr. Grandsire to consciousness. Dipping his handkerchief into the jug of water, he bathed the old man's face, and splashing some brandy into the glass, forced a few drops of the spirit between his lips. The treatment had an almost immediate effect. A sobbing breath heralded his coming to, and then he opened his eyes. For a moment, he stared dazedly about him; and then, raising a hand weakly, he passed it across his forehead.

'What — what — what happened?' he stammered, looking vaguely at the dramatist. 'I — I feel very queer, very queer indeed.'

'You fainted,' said Lowe gently. 'Have some more of this.' He held out the glass and Mr. Grandsire took it, sipping at the contents. A look of recognition came into his eyes as he set it down with a trembling hand.

'I — I remember,' he faltered. 'Yes, I remember. We — we were talking about — about someone called Nottingham Deane . . . '

'That's right. But don't worry about that now. Wait until you feel stronger.'

'I feel all right, Mr. Lowe,' said Grandsire, and his voice was more under control. 'I'm very sorry to have been such a fool, but I'm subject to these attacks. It's my heart, I think. Nothing radically wrong, you understand, but just a little weak. That — that dreadful discovery upstairs upset me . . . '

Lowe was silent. It had not been the discovery of the murder which had upset the old man, he was sure of that. It had been the mention of the name Nottingham Deane.

Mr. Grandsire leaned back in his chair, his face drawn and haggard, but otherwise almost completely recovered. 'You were

154

speaking,' he said hesitantly, 'about tracing a man called Nottingham Deane . . . '

'I was. I'm under the impression that you'll be able to help me.'

Mr. Grandsire shook his head. 'I don't know what gave you that impression, sir. But I assure you I know nothing of Mr. Deane. The name is unknown to me.'

'That's very extraordinary,' said Lowe, 'because I understand that Mr. Nottingham Deane arranged with his solicitors to transfer nearly three hundred thousand pounds from his account to yours.'

The old man started slightly, and the scared look that Lowe had surprised in his eyes before reappeared. 'Now you mention it,' he said, choosing his words carefully, 'I remember, of course. The name had — had slipped my memory. Yes, I had a business transaction with Mr. Deane some years ago through his solicitor, but that's all I know about him.'

'You never met him?' asked Lowe.

Again the old man shook his head. 'No, I never met him.'

'What was this business transaction which involved such a large sum?'

155

enquired the dramatist, and there was a perceptible pause before Mr. Grandsire answered.

'It — it concerned some property,' he said evasively at last. 'It's entirely a private matter, Mr. Lowe, and really, I don't see what authority you have for putting these questions to me.'

'I have no authority at all,' declared the dramatist candidly, 'other than that I'm trying to assist the police to discover the man responsible for these 'silver bell murders', and I believe that Nottingham Deane can help me, if I can find him.'

Mr. Grandsire looked at him, and now there was no doubt about the fear in his eyes.

'I — I don't quite understand,' he murmured. 'Are you suggesting that Mr. Nottingham Deane is the murderer?'

'I'm suggesting nothing,' said Lowe a little coldly. 'I'm merely making enquiries. In my opinion there is no doubt that Nottingham Deane, or whatever his real name is, is very closely connected with these crimes, and therefore I'm anxious to trace him; and when I learned that he had transferred three hundred thousand pounds from his account to yours, I was naturally under the impression that you'd be able to help me. I'm still under that impression.'

'I'm afraid I can't. And I'm sure you are labouring under a mistake. I can't believe that Nottingham Deane can have anything to do with this terrible business.'

'How can you say that when you've never met the man and know nothing about him?'

For a moment the old man was non-plussed. 'That's true,' he said reluctantly. 'Put it down to instinct, or whatever you like, Mr. Lowe, but I'm convinced that Nottingham Deane is unlikely to be mixed up with these crimes.'

'Have you any idea who is?' said the dramatist sharply.

'I?' Mr. Grandsire raised his eyebrows in a creditable imitation of surprise. 'My dear sir, how should I know? You surely don't imagine for one moment that I have any knowledge of these dreadful murders?'

Lowe more than imagined it. In his

own mind, he was certain that the man before him could supply vital information concerning the bell murders if he liked. That he was lying was obvious to the meanest intelligence, and lying very badly and unconvincingly.

'Are you acquainted,' he said, abruptly changing the subject, 'with a lady named Gloria Swayne?'

The question was unexpected, and Mr. Grandsire started. 'I've heard of her, of course,' he answered. 'Who hasn't? But I can't say I'm acquainted with her.'

'I was wondering,' continued Lowe, 'if you're aware of a contract Nottingham Deane got her to sign over four years ago. It was an extraordinary contract, offering her fifty thousand pounds in cash and the leading part in a new film, provided she undertook not to marry for a period of five years.'

'I know nothing about it,' declared Mr. Grandsire quickly. 'Nothing about it at all. It's entirely useless you questioning me concerning this man Deane. I've already told you that my relationship with him was purely a matter of business, and conducted entirely by correspondence. Beyond that, I know nothing about him!'

Lowe eyed him steadily, softly caressing his chin. It was the old man's eyes that dropped first. 'I'm sorry,' he said. 'I was hoping you'd be able to help me, Mr. Grandsire. Perhaps you'll tell me who your visitor was this afternoon?'

Mr. Grandsire moved uneasily in his chair. 'Really,' he protested, 'I can't see why you should be interested in a friend of mine who called quite by chance, a gentleman I hadn't seen for a number of years.'

'Mr. Grandsire,' said Lowe, and there was a perceptible change in his voice; it was harder and sterner, 'a few hours ago a man was killed in this place. He was killed by the same person responsible for the deaths of five other men. Anyone who was on the premises is naturally of interest to the police.'

'But my friend can have nothing to do with the killing of this unfortunate man Simmons,' said Mr. Grandsire. 'He was with me the entire time he was here, and left with me. We had some tea together, and I saw him on his train back to London.'

'Then there can be no objection on your part,' said the dramatist, 'to giving me his name.'

'Only,' answered Mr. Grandsire, 'that I should prefer to keep my friend out of this unpleasant business if possible.'

'You'll find that very difficult,' remarked Lowe. 'I assure you, Mr. Grandsire, that the police will want to know all about this man, and if you don't tell me, you'll have to tell them.'

The old man considered, frowning. 'Very well. His name is Collins. I knew him some years ago; he lives in Scotland. He was in London on business and called in to see me. That's all.'

Another lie, thought Lowe. *You made that story up on the spur of the moment, my friend.* 'What's Mr. Collins's address?' he said aloud.

Mr. Grandsire shook his head. 'I'm afraid I can't tell you that, because I don't know. He lives somewhere in — in Glasgow, I believe, but I don't know where.'

'Where's he staying while he's in

London?' said the dramatist relentlessly.

'He didn't tell me. You'll understand, Mr. Lowe, that we had several things to talk about, and he wasn't with me very long.'

'It seems peculiar, all the same,' commented Lowe, 'that although he was sufficiently friendly with you to come out to Stepney to pay you a visit, he should have omitted to give you an address that would find him if you wanted to communicate with him.'

'He may have been under the impression that I knew his address. Surely you're worrying a great deal over something that's of very little importance?'

'It's impossible to judge its importance! I'm afraid the police will go further into this matter, Mr. Grandsire. In fact, I have no doubt they'll wish to trace this man Collins.'

'I can tell you no more than I've told you,' was the stubborn reply as the old man rose a little unsteadily to his feet. 'And now I must ask you to close this interview, Mr. Lowe. I'm feeling far from well, and I must rest. If the police wish to see me, I'd esteem it a favour if you'd ask them to postpone it until later.'

There was no denying that he looked ill, and in spite of his conviction that he was keeping vital information back, Lowe felt sorry for him. 'Here's my card, Mr. Grandsire,' he said, taking his wallet from his pocket and extracting a slip of pasteboard. 'If by any chance you should remember anything concerning Nottingham Deane that you think might help me to find him, I should be glad if you'd communicate with me.'

The old man took the card, glanced at it, and laid it on his blotting pad. 'If such a contingency should arrive,' he answered, 'you can rest assured, Mr. Lowe, that I'll communicate with you at once.'

On this the interview ended, and leaving the office, Lowe went in search of Superintendent Jameson. That individual had completed his preliminary investigations and was on the point of sending Cosh Willis to fetch Mr. Grandsire.

'I should postpone any questions you want to put to him until later,' said Lowe. 'This business has upset him very badly, and he's having a rest.'

Jameson looked dubious. 'There are several things I wanted to ask him,' he muttered. 'I'm interested to know who this man was who called this afternoon to see him.'

'His name was Collins. He's an old friend of Grandsire's and lives in Scotland.' He repeated what the old man had told him.

The superintendent pursed his lips. 'That doesn't help us very much. All right, Willis, you needn't bother your master. I'll come back later and see him.'

Two uniformed men carrying a hand ambulance arrived at that moment, and the body of the unfortunate Simmons was lifted from the bed on to the stretcher and carried out.

'I shall want you to attend the inquest, Mr. Lowe,' said Jameson as they followed the remains downstairs. 'I expect it'll be the day after tomorrow, but I'll notify you.'

The news of the murder at the Prov had in some remarkable way spread round the district, and a crowd of people had gathered at the entrance when they left. The first of the reporters that later were to swarm like flies round the mission arrived as Lowe was taking his leave of Jameson. Leaving the superintendent to cope with the newspapermen, the dramatist made his way back to Portland Place, and during the journey his mind was occupied with the mysterious Mr. Collins.

There had been a large dictionary on Mr. Grandsire's desk, and he had noticed the old man's eyes stray towards it when he had asked the name of his visitor. He wondered whether it was a coincidence, or whether the name of the publisher of that dictionary had supplied Grandsire with the name he had mentioned.

15

A Job for White

When he reached his flat, he found White seated before the fire in the study reading a book. He laid aside the novel and looked up at his employer's entrance.

'Hello!' greeted Lowe. 'How long have you been back?'

'A couple of hours,' answered Arnold. 'I should have got here before, only just as I was leaving the hotel to catch the train, Inspector Halford sent up from the police station and asked me to drop in and see him. He wanted a signed statement, and also to subpoena me for the inquest.'

'When is it?'

'The day after tomorrow. It means another trip to Manchester.'

'Probably I'll come with you,' said his employer. He filled his pipe, lit it, and dropped into a chair. 'Now tell me all

165

about this Taverner business. You only gave me a very sketchy account on the telephone.'

Arnold complied, and Lowe listened without comment until he had finished.

'You think this man who trapped you in the empty house was Nottingham Deane?' he asked.

The secretary nodded. 'I don't see who else it could have been. My idea is that in some way or other he got wind of the fact that I'd gone to Manchester, followed me to the theatre, and heard what Taverner said about the envelope. It would've been quite easy for anyone to hear if they'd been loitering about outside the stage door.'

Lowe frowned thoughtfully through the smoke that curled upwards from the bowl of his pipe. If, as he believed, Grandsire and Nottingham Deane were one and the same person, it would be interesting to know whether the old man had been at the mission on the night that Taverner had met his death. If he had not, then there was a distinct possibility that he had been the man whom White had fought with in the house in Hulme Road. At the same time, he could scarcely reconcile his secretary's description of that mysterious individual with Grandsire's age. The man, according to White, had been abnormally strong; and although Grandsire looked fit for his age, it was hardly likely that his physical condition was good enough to put up a successful fight against a young man like White. In which case, who had been the masked man at Manchester?

Was he speaking the truth when he denied being Nottingham Deane? Unless he had in reality been Grandsire, it would appear so, for Lowe was convinced in his own mind that the eccentric old man who ran the East End Mission and the mysterious individual who had made that extraordinary proposition to Gloria Swayne were one and the same. The transfer of the money proved that, in his opinion. But if this was the case, then the bell murderer was not Nottingham Deane.

It was all very puzzling; and in spite of the knowledge he so far possessed, there was still a lot that remained to be discovered before he could legitimately call the problem solved.

He said nothing to Arnold White of the unfortunate Mr. Bookham's strange hobby, or the result it had led to. There was a secretive strain in his nature which made it impossible for him to produce a half-finished result. Until he had everything at his fingertips, he liked to keep his discoveries to himself, divulging them at the right moment and making everything clear. This trait in his character was partly due to the strong dramatic instinct his profession had instilled in him; a liking for bringing about a surprise denouement; and although it was very irritating to the people who worked with him, they had grown sufficiently used to the habit to more or less accept it with resignation. Therefore, although White enquired what progress he was making, he was not unprepared for the evasive answer which he got.

'Things are going fairly well,' said the dramatist. 'I think I've managed to make a little headway.' He mentioned his visit to the solicitors and the tracing of Simmons which had led him to the Providence Mission, and the tragedy that had resulted. 'I want you to watch this man Grandsire,' he concluded. 'Put on some old clothes and make yourself look as much like a loafer as possible. Keep an eye on the mission and follow this old man wherever he goes.'

'You think he's Nottingham Deane?' asked Arnold.

Lowe nodded. 'I'm pretty sure of it.'

'But what reason could he have for making that contract with Gloria Swayne?'

'Of that I haven't the least idea. It's one of the things I'd be very interested to know. This latest murder, however, should relieve her mind. Simmons, so far as I know, had no connection with her at all, and therefore neither directly nor indirectly can the motive for his murder be traced to her.'

'When do you want me to go?'

'As soon as possible,' replied the dramatist. 'It's my belief that Grandsire will make some effort to get in touch with the unknown man who called at the mission this afternoon, and he's the person I'm anxious to get in touch with.'

Arnold rose to his feet. 'I'll clear off at once,' he said.

'I'll arrange with Shadgold for someone to relieve you during the night,' said Lowe as he crossed to the door.

The secretary nodded and made his way to his bedroom, where he searched in the wardrobe for a sufficiently old suit that would fit the part he was undertaking. He found one, changed rapidly, and with the aid of a little soot from the chimney succeeded in transforming himself into a very creditable counterfeit of an out-of-work loafer.

'Will this do?' he asked a few seconds later, presenting himself for Lowe's inspection, and his employer nodded, approvingly.

'Excellent!' he said. 'If anything of importance occurs, you can telephone me.'

White took his departure, and for some time after he had gone, Lowe sat smoking thoughtfully, turning over in his mind the salient points that were bothering him. Presently he rose to his feet, knocked the ashes out of his pipe, and putting on his hat and coat went out.

Hailing a taxi, he gave the address of a

block of flats off Piccadilly, and a few minutes later was set down at the imposing entrance. Gloria Swayne occupied an apartment on the third floor, and a trim maid opened the door at his ring. He presented his card, and the woman, ushering him into the hall, went away in search of her mistress. She returned almost immediately. The dramatist was conducted into a small but tastefully furnished sitting-room where Gloria was talking to Mr. Shuberg.

'Come in, Mr. Lowe,' she said, rising to her feet, and she introduced him to the film director.

Mr. Shuberg's fat and florid face was lined with worry. His eyes had the appearance of weariness that comes from mental anxiety, and the hand that held a half-smoked cigar trembled slightly.

'It's nice of you to call, Mr. Lowe,' said Gloria. 'Have you anything to tell me?'

'Yes.' The dramatist seated himself in the chair she indicated. 'I want to set your mind at rest concerning the matter you mentioned the other day.'

'You — you mean about the murders?'

she asked in a low voice.

He nodded. 'You need no longer be afraid that they have any connection with you personally. Another was committed this afternoon, a man who I'm sure you couldn't possibly have had any acquaintance with.'

'Another?' said Mr. Shuberg. 'Good God! Where did this happen, Mr. Lowe?'

'In the East End, at a place run as a mission by a man called Grandsire.'

'Who — who was killed?' asked Gloria.

'An unfortunate out-of-work clerk named Simmons,' said Lowe. 'He was killed in the dormitory, and the little silver token was pinned on him.'

There was relief on Gloria's face. 'Thank heaven!' she breathed. 'I'm terribly sorry, of course, for the poor man, but you don't know what a weight you've taken off my mind.'

'I always told you,' said Mr. Shuberg, 'that you were worrying yourself unnecessarily. I never believed for a moment that these crimes had anything to do with that ridiculous contract you signed four years ago.'

'I know you didn't,' she said. 'But it seemed so strange that all the people who were killed were connected in some way with me. I was afraid.'

'Well, you need fear no more,' said Lowe. 'You can take my word for it, Miss Swayne, that although I believe there's a connection between that contract and the bell murders, it's not the one you thought.'

'You think there *is* a connection?' said Mr. Shuberg quickly.

'I do,' Lowe answered. 'Although I admit I haven't the least idea what it is.'

'Have you any idea,' said the film director, 'who's responsible for these crimes?'

'At the present, no, but I'm working on a theory I hope will shortly yield results.'

Mr. Shuberg was interested, but Lowe had no wish to discuss the matter, and turned the conversation into another channel. He had been considering seeking an interview with the film director, and finding him at Gloria Swayne's apartment seemed providential.

'Reverting to the contract which the

173

unknown Nottingham Deane persuaded Miss Swayne to sign four years ago,' he said, 'do you know anything about it?'

Mr. Shuberg raised his eyebrows. 'Me?' he said in surprise. 'What should I know about it, Mr. Lowe? I know the general terms, of course, but apart from that, nothing.'

'I was wondering whether you had any connection with this film in which he guaranteed Miss Swayne the leading part.'

Shuberg shook his head. 'No, I had nothing to do with it at all. I was, as a matter of fact, not in the film business in England at that time. I only came over from America three years ago.'

'And you've never heard of Nottingham Deane in connection with films?' persisted Lowe.

'No. I'd never heard the name at all until Gloria mentioned the contract to me.'

'Was Mr. Deane interested in films?' she enquired.

'Very much so,' said the dramatist. 'I've made one or two enquiries concerning him, and I understand that most of his money was invested in film companies.'

'D'you mean,' she asked quickly, 'that you've succeeded in discovering who he is?'

He smiled ruefully. 'Unfortunately, no. But I've found the solicitors who drew up your contract. Nottingham Deane, according to them, seems to be a very mysterious person. Perhaps — ' He turned to Shuberg. ' — the name Jonathan Grandsire is more familiar to you?'

'No,' said the film director. 'Should it be, Mr. Lowe?'

'I was wondering,' said the dramatist, and Gloria uttered an exclamation.

'I've heard it somewhere,' she said, wrinkling her brows. 'Now where? I thought it sounded familiar when you mentioned it before. I know!' The puzzled frown left her face. 'He's the father of one of the clerks at my solicitor's.'

It was Lowe's turn to be surprised. 'Are you sure?' he asked.

She nodded quickly. 'Positive! At least, he's not actually his father, he adopted him when he was a boy. He came to see me the other day on business. His name's Ronald Lane, and we got chatting and he told me all about it.'

Lowe digested this fresh piece of information. How did this adopted son of Mr. Grandsire's fit in? Had he anything to do with the strange business? Lowe ran over in his mind quickly what he knew so far, but could not find a place for Ronald Lane. He asked the name of Gloria's solicitors, and when she told him, he made a mental note of it. He decided that it would be interesting to meet Ronald Lane, though he never guessed how soon and under what strange circumstances that meeting was to take place.

16

Mr. Willis to the Rescue

A taxi carried Arnold White to the outskirts of Stepney, and half a mile from the station he stopped it and got out, considering it better to continue the rest of the way on foot. In that unsalubrious district, a taxi was an event, and to go too near the mission in it was asking for comment, which was the last thing he desired. His one ambition was to draw as little attention to himself as possible.

Adopting the slouching gait of the habitual loafer, he set off towards his objective. The night was dark and cloudy, and there was a dampness in the air that hinted at coming rain. He arrived at the corner of the street in which the Providence Mission was situated, and was turning into it when the sound of muffled shouts and oaths attracted his attention. There was a small public house on the corner, and as he paused to see what the row was about, the door of the bar burst open, and from its lighted interior a tangled knot of struggling men swayed out into the roadway. Arnold caught a glimpse of a blue helmet above the fighting mass, and concluded that some of the inhabitants of the district were having trouble with the law.

The yelling, shouting throng reeled backwards and forwards on the pavement. 'Get the rozzer!' screamed a shrill voice, and Arnold saw a man dart into the middle of the melee and swing a loaded stick at the back of the constable's head. It reached its mark, and with a strangled cry the policeman slumped to his knees and collapsed in the gutter.

White wasn't standing for this. Before the knot of roughs could sort themselves out, he was halfway across the street. A big burly brute of a man had drawn back his foot to kick the unconscious policeman when Arnold let him have it, full on the point of the jaw. With a grunt, he staggered backwards among his friends.

'Cosh 'im, 'Arry!' snarled a voice

viciously, and Arnold put up his arm just in time to ward off a blow aimed at his head by the man who had laid out the constable. He swung round and his left caught his attacker a smashing blow on the mouth. The man reeled away, spitting and cursing, and then the others closed in on him. White lashed out at the vicious faces, but the odds were against him. A blow caught him on the side of the head that sent him spinning into the road.

'Poke yer nose into wot doesn't concern yer, would yer, you — ' growled a voice. 'I'll learn yer!'

The speaker raised an empty beer bottle, a weapon he had probably grabbed from the bar during the commotion, and it might have gone hard with Arnold had not a hoarse Cockney voice interfered.

''Ere, Ted Brownlow, stop that!'

The man called Ted Brownlow swung round. 'What d'you want to interfere for, Cosh?' he snarled. 'This ain't your business!'

'We'll see whether it's my business or not, my old cock sparrer!' cried Mr. Willis. 'You leave that feller alone!' He forced his way through the knot of roughs and stood by Arnold, his hands clenched. 'Go on, beat it! All of yer!' he snapped. 'Ain't the place got a bad enough name without you makin' it worse! Go on, clear off!'

A muttered grumbling came from the little crowd of roughs; and then, whether it was on account of Mr. Willis's belligerent attitude, or because the constable was showing signs of returning consciousness and fumbling for his whistle, it was difficult to say, but the whole lot of them sheered off.

His rescuer bent down. 'Feelin' all right, mate?' he asked.

'Yus, thanks,' answered Arnold in a voice suitable for the type he was impersonating. 'I got a nasty packet, but it might 'ave been worse.'

'It might 'ave been a blinkin' sight worse!' said Mr. Willis cheerfully. 'Those perishers ain't 'alf a tough lot. 'Ere, come on,' he said, as a shrill blast from the constable's whistle signified that he had succeeded in applying it to his lips. 'We don't want to get mixed up with no trouble.'

Seeing what had happened, Arnold thought this was rather late, but he guessed that his rescuer meant trouble with the law. With Mr. Willis' help, he struggled to his feet.

'I live round 'ere,' said Cosh, waving his hand as if to indicate that he was lord of the local manor. 'You'd better come along with me and sit down for a while. From the sock that feller give yer, yer 'ead mustn't 'alf be ringin'.'

White agreed gratefully, as he felt a little shaky, and accompanied the stocky figure of his companion up the street just as thudding footsteps in the distance announced the arrival of reinforcements in answer to the constable's signal.

'It's a common place, that pub,' said Mr. Willis loftily, jerking his head back the way they had come. 'You wouldn't think they'd allow it, wot with the Flyin' Squad and coppers wot go to college. Still, I suppose they knows where to look when there's any trouble darn this way. It's a good job I 'appened to be takin' a breather, otherwise you'd 'a been for it. Ted Brownlow and 'Arry Pierce are 'ot

181

stuff. Not but wot you didn't ask for it,' he added. 'I don't 'old with 'elpin' a flatty! Wot d'yer want to interfere for?'

'One man against 'alf a dozen ain't sportin',' answered Arnold.

Mr. Willis sniffed. 'You can't afford to be sportin' with the perlice. Not that wot I've got anythin' against them now, I've give all that up. I used to be a bit of a lad, but I'm runnin' straight.' He stopped outside the door of the Providence Mission, to the secretary's surprise, and jerked his thumb towards the doorway. 'This is where I 'ang out,' he said. 'Come on in.'

White followed him up the steps and into the big hall. 'You must be Cosh Willis,' he said as his new friend opened the door of his little office.

Mr. Willis beamed genially. ''Eard of me, 'ave yer? Yus, I'm Cosh Willis, pretty well known about these parts. Sit down and 'ave a fag.' Arnold took one and lit it. Lowe had mentioned Cosh Willis when he had given him an account of the murder, and the secretary had guessed who he was as soon as he had turned into the Mission. Here was a piece of luck that was heaven-sent.

'Wot's yer name?' asked Mr. Willis affably, perching himself on the corner of the small table.

'Gibbs,' replied Arnold, improvising quickly. 'Charlie Gibbs.'

'D'yer live round 'ere?' enquired Cosh, trickling smoke through his wide nostrils.

Arnold shook his head. 'No, I don't live nowhere — not now.'

Mr. Willis looked sympathetic. 'Down on yer luck, are yer? What's yer lay?'

'Anythin' that'll bring in a bit of dough. I ain't perticlar.'

'Ever been in trouble?'

'No, I've always run straight. Might be better off than wot I am at the moment if I 'adn't.'

'That's right,' said Mr. Willis virtuously. 'Honesty pays in the long run. Look at me. I used to be a bad character, I did, but I realised the error of me ways and now I've got a good job and can 'old me 'ead up with any man. Would yer like a bit of grub?'

'Not 'alf!' said White. 'You ain't 'alf a

good sort, mister!'

'Wait there,' said Mr. Willis, and he went out. He returned after a short delay with a hunk of bread and cheese, and a mug of cocoa. 'Get that inside yer,' he said magnanimously, setting it down in front of White, and watching while he ate voraciously. 'Got anywhere to kip tonight?' he asked presently.

Arnold, his mouth full, shook his head.

'You can doss 'ere if you like,' said Mr. Willis generously. 'The guv'nor 'ull be pleased to let yer stay.'

'Oo's 'e?' asked White, although he knew very well.

'Bloke called Grandsire,' answered Cosh. ''E's a good feller but a bit eccentric. We 'ad some trouble 'ere this afternoon and it's given 'im a bad turn.'

'Wot sort of trouble?'

'The 'Big Thing',' replied Cosh seriously. 'Feller wot was stayin' 'ere was bumped off by that chap wot sticks them little bell things on the people 'e rubs out. It give me a bit of a ginger-up, I can tell yer!'

He launched into a highly coloured

account of the tragedy, and Arnold listened, suitably impressed.

'Blimey!' he said. 'Nasty thing to 'ave 'appened!'

'It were!' agreed Mr. Willis. 'Nothin' like that sort of thing fer gettin' a place a bad name. We ain't 'ad any trouble 'ere before, leastways, not real trouble. We 'ad a woman come 'ere once whose 'usband was in stir fer knockin' 'er about, which 'e used ter do regl'ar, and she was sittin' downstairs one evenin' when 'er old man come in; 'e'd been released that day, 'e 'ad. Comes up to 'er and fetches 'er a four-penny one across the face. Luckily I 'appened to be in the room, otherwise I believe 'e'd 'ave done 'er in. I pasted 'im good and proper, and they 'ad to fetch an ambulance to take 'im to the police station.' He smiled reminiscently. 'We don't get much of that, though,' he added sadly, 'that was the only time.' He threw the end of his cigarette into the fireplace. 'I'll go and arrange with the guv'nor about you stoppin',' he said. 'You needn't worry, it's only a matter of form, 'e leaves most of the arrangin' to me.'

With this completely untrue statement, he left the office; and Arnold, gulping the remainder of his cocoa, leaned back in his chair and congratulated himself on his good luck, for good luck it undoubtedly was. When he had started on his mission, he had visualised a cold and uncomfortable vigil; and now he not only had a better chance of keeping an eye on Grandsire, but he would do so in comparative comfort. Somehow or other he would have to get in touch with Lowe, let him know what had happened, and prevent him making arrangements with Shadgold. There was no need now for anyone to relieve him.

Mr. Willis returned, his ugly face one huge grin. 'That's all right,' he said, with satisfaction. 'You can stay 'ere for a couple of nights if yer likes.'

'I'm glad I met you, mate,' said Arnold gratefully.

Mr. Willis made a gesture with a stubby and not over-clean hand. 'That's all right,' he said. 'I like a feller wot's a bit 'andy with 'is fists.'

'Can I pop out and get some

cigarettes?' enquired the secretary, hoping that this would provide him with an opportunity for telephoning to his employer.

'Course you can,' said Mr. Willis. 'Wot d'yer think this is, a bloomin' prison? This ain't a Government institootion. We don't put no restrictions on the people wot stays 'ere, except that they 'as to be in by ten o'clock. You pop out and get yer fags — the shop's at the end of the road — and when you come back, I'll show you over the place.'

Arnold popped out, found the shop which Mr. Willis had mentioned, bought three packets of Woodbines, and went in search of a public telephone. He found a call box near the station and got through to Portland Place. Lowe was out, but he left a message with the housekeeper explaining what had happened, and having assured himself that the woman had written it down correctly, returned to the mission.

Mr. Willis was waiting for him and proceeded to conduct him round the premises. He showed him the big dining-room where some ten men of varying ages and types were warming themselves in front of a big fire or attending to odd jobs. It was very similar to an ordinary lodging-house, except that everything was spotlessly clean and there was a wholesome smell of disinfectant about. Nobody took any notice of them, and they passed up the stairs where Arnold caught a glimpse of one or two tiny bedrooms, each with a white quilt on the truckle bed and white painted furniture.

'Them's for the women,' explained his guide. 'They shoves the men in 'ere.' He opened the door to a dormitory, and Arnold peered into the long room.

'Was this where that chap was bumped off?' he asked, and Mr. Willis nodded.

'Yus,' he answered. 'In that bed over there. We've put a screen round it. You'll be sleepin' in 'ere tonight.' He closed the door and pointed to a flight of stairs that led out of the passage almost opposite the dormitory. 'That leads to the guv'nor's quarters,' he remarked. 'And that little room at the end of the passage is where I 'angs out.'

They went back to the hall, and after chatting for a little while longer in Mr.

Willis's office, Arnold yawned and suggested that he would like to go to bed.

'Go along,' said Mr. Willis. 'You can 'ave the bed near the door or the centre one on the left 'and side. Neither of them's in use.'

Arnold decided on the one near the door, and saying good night to his new acquaintance, made his way up the stairs to the dormitory. Several of the inmates were preparing for slumber, a procedure that consisted of merely removing their boots and ragged jackets; and nobody took any notice of White as he followed suit and slipped between the coarse but clean sheets.

He had no intention of going to sleep, but he simulated slumber. A step he recognised as belonging to Mr. Willis passed the door, and then there was silence broken only by the heavy breathing of the men in the beds near him, punctuated occasionally by an unmusical snore.

In spite of his determination to keep awake, he began to feel a drowsiness steal over him; the warmth of the bed and his exertions of the day combined to produce a longing for sleep which was almost overpowering. Several times he found himself dozing, and startled to wakefulness with an effort. This would never do, he thought. If he fell asleep, anything might happen.

He slipped out of bed softly, went over to one of the washstands, and making as little noise as possible, poured some water into a tin basin and bathed his face. The shock of the cold water cleared the sleep from his brain, and drying himself on a towel, he went back and sat on the edge of his bed. And as he did so, he heard a sound: the faint, unmistakable shuffle of footsteps, followed by the creak of a loose board. It came from outside the passage, from the direction of the narrow stairway that led up to Mr. Grandsire's apartment.

He listened, holding his breath in order to hear more clearly. The footsteps passed the dormitory door and faded into silence. Cautiously he rose to his feet, crept to the door, and opened it, peering out into the dark passage. Whoever it was who was moving about had gone down

190

the stairs to the floor below. He tiptoed along the corridor and, leaning over the banister, peered down into the hall beneath. A faint light glimmered, its origin obscured by the staircase; and then a candle came into view, held in the hand of a white-haired man whom he guessed at once was Mr. Grandsire.

The old man was fully dressed, and as Arnold looked, he set the candle down on a table in the big hall, and reaching up to a rack, took down an overcoat and hat. There was a suggestion of secrecy about his every movement that impressed Arnold with a sense of furtiveness. Obviously he was going out. When he had put on his hat and coat, he crossed to the door and began to pull back the heavy bolt. The secretary felt the wave of cold air that blew in as the door was opened. The old man came back, extinguished the candle, and in the darkness that followed, Arnold heard the gentle thud of the heavy front door close.

Instantly he hurried down the stairs, moving without a sound, and at the foot he paused and listened. But hearing nothing, he took a torch from his pocket and risked switching on the light. Flashing it round, he saw, as he had expected, that the hall was empty. Mr. Grandsire had gone on his midnight excursion.

17

Startling News

Trevor Lowe found the secretary's message when he reached home after his interview with Gloria Swayne. Mr. Shuberg had walked part of the way with him for the purpose, as he soon discovered, of expressing his views concerning a certain theory he held with regard to the contract she had signed.

'I haven't said anything to Miss Swayne,' he said confidentially, 'but it's my impression that this man Nottingham Deane caused that contract to be drawn up for no other purpose than because he'd seen her somewhere and fallen in love with her.'

Lowe was sceptical. 'It hardly seems to me the best way to express one's affection,' he remarked dryly. 'He only appeared once and has kept out of the way ever since.'

'He's probably one of those eccentric fellows,' said Mr. Shuberg, refusing to have his idea lightly set aside. 'There's no other explanation for that marriage clause. He put that in to prevent any other fellow trespassing on his preserves. Maybe when the five years are up he'll come forward and offer a proposal of marriage himself.'

The dramatist was not impressed.

'Perhaps,' said the film director when he had discounted the idea, 'you can suggest some other explanation?'

Lowe could have suggested half a dozen which would cover the facts, none of which he believed was the true one, but he refrained because he had no wish to be inveigled into an argument on the subject. He left Mr. Shuberg at Piccadilly Circus and walked up Oxford Street home. It was not his nearest way, but he was in no hurry, and the exercise helped the working of his brain.

He had barely read White's message and settled down to a pipe and his thoughts when the telephone bell rang and Shadgold's voice came over the wire.

'Hello, Mr. Lowe!' he said. 'I've just got back. That Taverner business is as much a mystery as any of the others. The murderer left no clue behind, and although the local authorities and I made a close inspection of the house where Mr. White was confined, we found nothing there of any value.'

'I didn't suppose you would,' said the dramatist. 'You're up against an extremely clever man, Shadgold.'

He heard the inspector grunt. 'I must say he moves pretty quickly. The first thing I heard when I got back was that there had been another murder.'

'Yes, I was present at the discovery,' said Lowe. 'You can cross Simmons off that list I gave you, Shadgold.' He heard a startled exclamation.

'Good Lord! Was Simmons one of them?' cried the inspector.

'He was,' replied Lowe grimly. 'And I should advise you to get on the track of the others as soon as possible and have them closely guarded, otherwise there'll be a few more you can cross off!'

'My sergeant's been attending to the

matter while I've been away. I'll hurry things up. By the way, you were enquiring about old Grandsire and the Providence Mission. Funny that this fresh crime should have happened there.'

'Most amusing,' said Lowe dryly. 'I'm glad you got a good laugh out of it.'

'There's no need to be sarcastic!' said Shadgold in an injured voice. 'How did you manage to be there when the discovery was made?'

'Because I was forestalling you and doing a little tracing up of these people on my own account. It was quite by accident I chose Simmons. Find out where those other people are living as soon as possible, and have them watched day and night!'

'I will,' promised Shadgold. 'You've nothing else to tell me, I suppose?'

Lowe smiled at this rather broad hint that the inspector would welcome a little further information. 'Nothing further at the moment,' he said, 'but I don't think it'll be long now before you'll know everything.'

He rang off before the inspector could

put any more questions, and going back to his chair, settled down once more to his thoughts. It was fairly late when he went to bed, having sketched out a mental plan of campaign. Up to the present, he had done everything he could to ensure that the bell man's activities should be checked. He had suggested who the other possible victims might be, and it was up to Scotland Yard to protect them. It was impossible for himself to attend to that; it was more than one man could do. He was considerably uneasy, all the same, for he knew, or thought he knew, the terrible danger in which the remaining seven people who had served on that jury, twenty-four years ago, were in.

If, he thought, as he lay in bed staring into the darkness of his room, he only knew which of them had been selected as the next victim, it would be easy. A close watch could be kept and the mysterious murderer taken red-handed. But there was no means of discovering this, and the only possible precaution that could be taken was to have them all closely guarded.

He fell asleep at last and slept

dreamlessly until he was awakened by his housekeeper with his early-morning tea. He got up at once, and when he had had his breakfast, set out to follow up the line of enquiry which he had mapped out the night before.

It took him to a dingy set of chambers in King's Bench Walk, and the grey-haired man who sat behind the big desk littered with brief and legal-looking documents greeted him with a smile of welcome as he was shown in by the clerk.

'Come in, Lowe,' he said cordially. 'It must be nearly nine months since I saw you. Been pretty busy, I suppose?'

'Fairly,' agreed the dramatist. 'And you?'

'Up to my eyes in it,' grunted Sir Everard Spencer. 'Work is the penalty of success, Lowe,' he chuckled. 'I suppose I needn't flatter myself that this is a friendly call?'

'I'm afraid not. I want to talk to you about a case which you have probably forgotten, although I believe it contributed considerably towards making your reputation.'

The stout K.C. eyed him enquiringly.

'What case do you refer to?' he asked.

'A case that happened twenty-four years ago,' said Lowe, 'in which you were the defending counsel. The Norwood murder.'

Sir Everard's thick lips pursed into a silent whistle. 'By Jove, that's going back a bit!' he said. 'Makes one feel old to resurrect that. What do you want to know about it?'

'Everything you can tell me. Particularly anything you know about the chief people concerned.'

The K.C. picked up a pipe from a tray in front of him and began to fill it methodically from a pouch which he took from his pocket. 'It was a fairly straightforward case,' he said after a pause. 'Though the verdict should never have been allowed, in my opinion. There's not the slightest doubt that the woman was crazy, although the medical experts disagreed. She should never have been hanged, but sent to Broadmoor. What's the idea of brushing the cobwebs off?'

Lowe looked at him gravely. 'I'll tell you,' he said, 'if you'll promise to regard what I'm going to say as confidential, at any rate for the moment.'

'Go ahead,' said Sir Everard, and he lit his pipe, puffing great clouds of smoke into the air.

Lowe 'went ahead', and to such purpose that long before he had finished what he had to say, the K.C. was staring at him, his pipe out and forgotten and his genial, florid face the picture of amazed incredulity.

18

The Half-forgotten Crime

For some seconds after he had finished speaking, there was silence in the dingy chambers, and then Sir Everard Spencer slowly exhaled a long breath.

'I thought my profession had rendered me immune from surprises,' he remarked gravely, 'but I must confess that you've given me the greatest surprise I've ever had in my life.'

'You think I'm right?' asked the dramatist.

The K.C. nodded vigorously. 'Unquestionably you're right! I don't think there can be any doubt about it. But the point, and a very important point, is, who is responsible?'

'That's where I was hoping you'd be able to help me.'

Sir Everard frowned and gently rubbed his chin. 'It's incredible,' he muttered, 'that after all these years there should be a repercussion. I remember the Norwood murder well. As you say, it contributed a great deal towards launching me on my career. What I can't understand is why this campaign of vengeance should have been delayed for so long.'

'That's one of my stumbling blocks,' admitted Lowe, 'but no doubt there's a very good reason.'

The crime to which the K.C. referred had, twenty-four years previously, filled the newspapers and caused a great deal of controversy. The murder of Douglas Bell had been a tragedy full of what editors and newspaper men call 'human interest'. Both the chief actors in the drama had been young. Douglas Bell was but twenty-seven at the time of his tragic death, and his wife Sylvia two years his junior. They had been married eighteen months and, as several witnesses testified at the trial, it would have been difficult to have found a happier couple. Everything that was necessary to make life a thing of joy they had: money, a lovely home, and a beautiful child of six months. Bell, in spite of his age, controlled a prosperous estate agency in the West End of London and was devoted to his family.

It was the nurse who looked after the child who made the terrible discovery. It was the custom, after the maid had brought Mr. and Mrs. Bell their early morning cup of tea, for this woman to bring the baby to the mother, and as usual on that fatal January morning she had done this. The screams of the child later brought her hurrying to the bedroom, and there she had found Douglas Bell dead in bed, with blood pouring from a wound in his throat, and his wife, a dazed expression on her face, bending over him, an open razor in her hand.

The horrified nurse called the police, and Sylvia Bell was arrested. She could make no coherent statement, and, indeed, seemed to be unconscious of what she had done. There was no doubt, however, concerning her guilt, for there was no one else in the bedroom, and no one else could possibly have been there.

The subsequent investigation by the

police revealed a fact which told heavily against her. The servants testified that she was subject to fits of ungovernable temper, and that two days before the murder she and her husband had quarrelled violently over a question of money.

The defence tried to prove that the crime had been committed during a brainstorm, and brought medical witnesses to testify to the fact that Sylvia Bell was not responsible for her actions. But the prosecution brought other witnesses of equal status who said that she was perfectly responsible. She had no parents living, only a brother who was abroad, and although Douglas Bell's father did his best for her, even to the extent of paying for her defence, the jury brought in a verdict of guilty after only three hours' deliberation, and she was sentenced to death.

The appeal which followed in due course was dismissed. Had a different home secretary been in office, this would probably not have happened, but Sir Victor Nash was a strong believer in capital punishment, and so the law eventually took its course.

Such, in brief, was the case which Lowe had discovered among the files in the newspaper office and which, as soon as he saw the name Sylvia Bell, had suggested a connection with the present series of apparently motiveless crimes.

'You're sure,' said Sir Everard, 'that these people who have been killed were on the jury?'

Lowe nodded. 'Yes, I looked up the Records at the Old Bailey,' he said. 'It was that which made me certain I was right.'

'Then so far as I can see, there's only one person who can be responsible for these killings.'

'You mean the brother?'

'Without a doubt! As I said just now, the woman ought never to have been hanged, there's not the slightest question about that. She was as mad as a hatter. Not outwardly, of course; outwardly she was just a normal pretty woman. But there's no doubt she had certain difficulties — probably hereditary; her father committed suicide. One of the finest alienists in the country told me, after he had examined her, that he was convinced she was not responsible for her actions and had no recollection of having killed her husband.'

'So that it's quite possible,' murmured Lowe, 'that there was madness in the family.'

'I think it's not only possible, but certain.'

'Then this brother is probably tarred with the same brush?'

'That's fairly obvious,' answered the K.C. 'No normal man would set out to commit a series of crimes such as these bell murders. I should say he was as crazy as a coot, although I don't suppose you'd know it even if you met him. This little token, the silver bell, is of course evidently intended to suggest Sylvia Bell.'

'Undoubtedly,' said Lowe. 'What happened to the child? Do you know?'

Sir Everard shook his head. 'I've no idea. I believe an aunt came forward and offered to adopt her, but I couldn't be sure. Why?'

'I'd like to trace the child,' said the dramatist thoughtfully. 'It was a woman, wasn't it?'

'Yes, and its Christian name was Ann, but that's all I can tell you. I don't mind saying, in my opinion, Lowe, that although I believe you're right concerning these Bell murders and that it's Sylvia Bell's brother who is responsible, you're going to have a tough job finding him.'

'I know that,' answered his friend. 'Like all abnormal people, he's possessed of supreme cunning. All the same, now that we know why and who the people are he's marked down for his victims, we can take adequate precautions. I've given the police the names of the remaining members of that jury and suggested that they should be closely guarded.'

'Have you told them why?'

'No, not yet. I want to get the whole thing cut and dried before I do that.' He paused, and then: 'What was Sylvia Bell's maiden name, do you remember?'

Sir Everard frowned in an effort of recollection. 'Something like Lant. No, I've got it! Lanter. Sylvia Lanter.'

'Did you meet the father of the dead man?'

'Yes — a fine chap! He was heartbroken

about his son, but he put up all the money for the defence because he was convinced that the unfortunate woman was mad.'

'What was he like?' said the dramatist, but the K.C.'s description was vague. 'The brother of course you never saw?'

'No,' replied Sir Everard. 'He was abroad.'

'The most puzzling thing,' said Lowe with knitted brows, 'is why all this time should have elapsed before he started his vengeance plan. There must be some explanation for that, and it might prove helpful.'

'If he was abroad, perhaps he didn't know anything about his sister's execution until recently.'

'That's possible, but it doesn't seem to me to be a sufficiently good explanation. His name would be Lanter. What's his Christian name?'

'That I can't tell you,' said the K.C. 'I don't think I ever heard it.'

'Well he's got to be found, and found before he can do any more damage.'

'The proverbial needle in a haystack would be easier to locate. You realise that this fellow has undoubtedly changed his name, and therefore you've got several million people to choose from.'

'I realise the difficulties,' said Lowe with a wry smile. 'Nobody more so, but I think they can be overcome. In the meantime, I should very much like to trace that child.'

'Why?' demanded Sir Everard Spencer, a little surprised. 'What's she got to do with it?'

'I think she may have a lot to do with it.'

An idea had occurred to him, an idea which he refrained from putting into words. If the child of Douglas and Sylvia Bell was still alive, she would now be a little over twenty-four — the same age as Gloria Swayne! Was it possible that Gloria Swayne and Ann Bell were one and the same? And if so, did this offer an explanation for the mysterious Nottingham Deane's interest in her, and provide a motive for that extraordinary contract he had persuaded her to sign?

19

Mr. Grandsire Disappears

Trevor Lowe left Sir Everard Spencer's chambers in the temple feeling a little disappointed at the meagre result of his interview. He had hoped that his visit would have been more profitable than it had; for much of the information the K.C. had been able to give him he already possessed. Certainly it was gratifying to find that such an eminent man as Sir Everard Spencer was in agreement with his theory concerning the connection between the present series of crimes and that twenty-four-year-old murder, but it did not extend the present situation any further.

Coming out into Fleet Street, he hailed a taxi and was driven to Gloria's flat. She was a little surprised to see him, but welcomed him with a smile. He was glad to notice that she looked considerably better than when he had seen her before.

The dark marks had gone from under her eyes, and the faint lines of worry between her level brows had been smoothed away.

'I'm sorry to worry you, Miss Swayne,' he said, accepting the chair she indicated, 'but I've come to see if you can give me a little information.'

'I'll do anything I can,' she answered. 'What is it you want to know?'

'It's occurred to me that the motive behind this contract you signed may lie in your past.'

Her forehead puckered doubtfully. 'How do you mean?'

'I mean that there must obviously be some reason for this man Nottingham Deane going to so much trouble and spending so much money to ensure that you wouldn't marry for a period of five years, and I'm wondering if we can't find that reason in something that might have happened during your childhood, or perhaps later.'

She shook her head. 'I know of nothing.'

'Who were your parents and where were you born?'

'I was born in London, but who my parents were I don't know. You see,' she went on quickly, 'they died when I was only a few months old, and I was adopted by an aunt.'

Lowe felt his heart beat a little faster. This fitted in with his theory that the woman before him was the child of Douglas and Sylvia Bell. Ann Bell had been adopted by an aunt, so much he had learnt from Sir Everard. 'Then,' he continued, 'Swayne is not your real name?'

She shook her head and smiled. 'It's a name I adopted for professional purposes. Most people on the stage take a name other than their own, a name more euphonious and suitable for billing and press purposes. I'm afraid my real name isn't very impressive.'

'Would you mind telling me what it is?'

She hesitated for a moment. 'Ann Briggs,' she said, with a grimace. 'You'll understand, Mr. Lowe, that it wasn't the kind of name likely to impress the general public.'

He agreed a little absently, for the fact

that Gloria's real Christian name was Ann proved to him that he was on the right track.

'Was Briggs the name of your parents?' he enquired, and she nodded.

'Yes. The aunt who adopted me was my father's sister.'

There had been no mention of a sister, thought Lowe, in the account of the trial; Douglas Bell's father had been mentioned, but there was no reference to any other relation. It was quite understandable why the child's name had been changed. No doubt the good lady who had adopted her after the tragic death of her father and mother had considered that it would be a handicap for her to go through life bearing such a notorious name as Bell, though they might, he thought, have chosen something a little more inspiring than Briggs.

'Do you remember anything of your childhood?' he asked.

'Very little,' she replied. 'I have a vague recollection of my aunt; an elderly thin-faced woman, rather old-fashioned in her ideas. She lived in a big house on

Brixton Hill, but as soon as I was old enough I was sent to a boarding school, and except for during the holidays I saw very little of her. I don't think,' she added, 'that she was very fond of me. It always seemed to me that she looked after me more from a sense of duty than anything else. Sometimes I caught her looking at me almost with dislike.'

'What was her name?'

'Alford,' replied Gloria. 'Clara Alford.'

'Is she alive now?'

'No, she died when I was fourteen. If she'd been alive, I should never have gone on the stage. She hated anything connected with it. But when she died, I had to do something. The small income on which she had lived ended at her death, and I was left practically destitute. Luckily I'd always been interested in dancing, and I managed to get into a juvenile troupe.'

'You don't remember anyone else,' he persisted, 'except Mrs. Alford?'

'Miss,' she corrected with a smile. 'Aunt Clara was a spinster. No, Mr. Lowe, I don't remember anyone else, except one or two elderly ladies who used to visit her now and again. It wasn't a very happy period of my life, and I've done my best to forget it.'

In his mind's eye, he could visualise the type of household in which she had been brought up, and mentally he agreed with her that it could not have been very joyous. The question was who Clara Alford had been. He was pretty sure she had not been Douglas Bell's sister. Bell had been a young man at the time of his death, and, from Gloria's account, Miss Alford had been an elderly woman. If she had not been Bell's sister, why had she told Gloria she was? In order to offer some excuse for her adoption; to give herself some kind of standing and so render her authority over the child more binding? This seemed a reasonable suggestion, but it didn't supply an answer to the original question — who was she? Nor was there anything in what he had learnt so far concerning Gloria Swayne's past to offer any suggestion for the motive that had prompted the unknown Nottingham Deane to draw up the contract.

He put a number of further questions to Gloria, but could elicit nothing that threw any more light on the matter. However, he had established one point, sufficiently at any rate to satisfy himself, that Gloria Swayne and little Ann Bell were one and the same.

Taking his leave, he walked back to his flat, hoping that there might be some message from White. But there was nothing further, and after he had had lunch he settled down to think over the result of his morning's work; and quite suddenly a suggestion came to him that explained the eccentric Nottingham Deane's frantic efforts to prevent Gloria Swayne from marrying.

The moment it occurred to him, he wondered why he hadn't thought of it before. It should have sprung instantly to his mind as soon as he had learned Gloria was Ann Bell; and, having discovered the motive, it was but a step to the real identity of Nottingham Deane.

He considered this fresh idea from every angle, and the more he considered it, the more certain he became that his theory was the right one. It had been obvious from the beginning that the contract had not been drawn up from any enmity to Gloria. On the contrary, it had, in one fell swoop, supplied her with a comfortable income for life and lifted her from the ruck of her profession to the top of the tree. Therefore Deane, acting as he had, had had her best interests at heart. The clause barring her marriage was also in her interest if the idea which had come to him was the true one.

And the person most likely to be interested in her welfare was the father of the murdered man. He felt that Sylvia Bell's brother could be discounted so far as Nottingham Deane was concerned. He was, without a doubt, thoroughly unbalanced and possessing the flaw that had so tragically appeared in his sister. It wouldn't be he who had striven to save Ann Bell from future worry; which only left Douglas Bell's father. And according to Lowe's preconceived idea, if Douglas Bell's father was Nottingham Deane, then Douglas Bell's father was Jonathan Grandsire; for he had made up his mind that Jonathan Grandsire and Nottingham Deane were one and the same.

Slowly the mists surrounding this extraordinary problem were dispersing. The various threads were knotting up, and he began to see on the fabric which had been so blank the vague outline of a design.

The next step was undoubtedly to tackle Grandsire and see what could be learned from him. The old man had been reticent at their previous interview, but probably if Lowe hinted at the extent of his knowledge, he would be more open. The fact that he called himself Grandsire did nothing to detract from Lowe's theory that he was Douglas Bell's father. Naturally he, too, would have changed his name, wishing to forget the tragic episode the newspapers had rendered world-notorious — to forget and be forgotten as having any connection with it.

His motive for having the child traced, and putting forward the proposition which he had, was so simple when all the facts were considered. He had known of the terrible illness that had existed in the mother and which, according to Sir Everard Spencer, had probably been hereditary. He had been afraid that it might appear sooner or later, in the daughter, and that a repetition of the dreadful crime which had startled the country might occur if Ann Bell should ever marry; and for this reason had inserted the marriage clause which had so puzzled Lowe. It all hung together — but why hadn't the old man revealed himself to Gloria? The answer to this was because he couldn't do so without divulging the whole story and letting her know who her parents were.

It had been a most considerate action on his part not to do this, for had he done so, she would have realised that the blood of a murderess ran in her veins, and there would have hung over her always the dread that that terrible taint which had caused Sylvia Bell to kill, unconsciously, the man she loved, might come out in herself. That, evidently, was the reason why 'Nottingham Deane' had come into existence, and why such elaborate precautions had been taken to ensure that his identity should never be discovered. He had realised that the strange contract he had proposed would cause a certain amount of curiosity, and that no doubt Gloria would make every effort to discover who he was; and so he had gone to an immense amount of trouble to obliterate his trail.

Lowe rose from the chair in which he had been musing and knocked the ashes out of his pipe. He was feeling intensely pleased with himself at having worked the whole thing out so neatly.

A glance at the clock told him that it was a quarter to three. A cab would take him to the Providence Mission in an hour, and he would be able to put his theory to the test. He was on the point of leaving the study to fetch his hat and coat when the telephone rang, and crossing to the desk, he picked up the receiver.

'Hello?' he called, expecting to hear his secretary's voice at the other end of the wire.

'Is that Mr. Lowe?' enquired a gruff voice, and when the dramatist had replied in the affirmative: 'Just a minute, sir;

Superintendent Jameson wants to speak to you.'

Lowe waited, and a few seconds later Jameson's voice reached his ears. 'Mr. Lowe?' said the local superintendent. 'You've let me in for a nice lot of trouble, sir!'

'Why? What have I done?' asked Lowe in surprise.

'You know you stopped me questioning Grandsire the other afternoon,' grunted the superintendent, 'because you said he wasn't well enough?'

'Well, what about it?'

'Well, now I can't question him at all! The man's gone!'

'Gone?' echoed Lowe, frowning.

'Yes, gone, sir!' repeated Jameson irritably. 'He left the Providence Mission some time during the night and has vanished into thin air!'

20

The Man in the Car

After that one quick glance round the empty hall, Arnold White switched out his torch and slipped noiselessly over to the front door. He was anxious to discover what lay behind this nocturnal excursion on the part of Mr. Grandsire; curious to learn where the old man had gone. He couldn't have got very far. Twisting the catch, Arnold pulled the heavy door open and stepped out into the cold and silent night, closing the portal gently behind him.

Thirty yards away from the entrance to the Providence Mission was a light standard, and he caught a glimpse of Grandsire as he passed through the circle of light cast by this illumination. He set off in pursuit.

The old man was walking quickly, and evidently had no fear of being followed, for he glanced neither to right nor left, but kept straight on down the street. At a side turning, he paused, and for the first time looked back. Arnold dodged into a doorway, and when he emerged, his quarry was no longer in sight. He guessed that he had turned the corner, and hurried towards the entrance of the other street. As he slowed up and peered cautiously round the wall of the end building, he caught sight of the dim lights of a standing car drawn up near the kerb a few yards away. There was no sign of Mr. Grandsire, but the murmur of voices came to his ears, and he concluded that the old man was talking to the owner of the car.

Who was it he had come to meet at this hour of the night? Someone, apparently, who had a particular reason for not wishing their presence known, otherwise they would have stopped openly at the mission and not remained lurking in a side turning.

Arnold was intensely curious. He would have given a lot to have been near enough to overhear that murmured conversation, but that was impossible. If he turned the corner, he would show himself, and yet it was essential that he should find out who the man was to whom Grandsire was talking.

He tried to think of a means by which he could do this without giving himself away, but nothing suggested itself, and then the murmur of voices ceased. To his straining ears there came a thin startled cry, followed a moment later by the slam of a door. The harsh whine of an electric starter jarred on the silence, blended with a rhythmic purr as the engine picked up and the car began to move towards him.

There had been no mistaking that sudden cry. Grandsire had been attacked by the man he had come to meet, and had either been left dead or dying on the pavement or had been pulled into the car, which was now gathering speed.

Arnold thought quickly. This was a crisis that had to be tackled instantly. Fate had thrown into his hands a chance that was never likely to come again. It was essential that he should not let that car go with its unknown occupant without trying to discover who he was and whither he was bound.

A quick glance at the spot where it had been standing showed him that there was no sign of Grandsire, conscious or unconscious; and then as the machine reached the corner, he saw his opportunity and seized it. It was a powerful two-seater coupe with a long raking back containing a dickey seat which was closed. It swung round, and as it did so he raced after it, and with a spring landed on the sloping surface of the back. He nearly slid off, but by clutching the right wing and jamming his foot against the rear bumper, he managed to retain his hold. He wondered whether the driver had felt the shock of his landing. Apparently he had not, or if he had, he had put it down to the unevenness of the surface of the road.

The car continued on its way, its speed increasing momentarily. Through the deserted street of Stepney, along the Whitechapel Road to Aldgate sped the car, past the Bank and into High Holborn, through Russell Square and on past Hampstead and Golder's Green.

Arnold's body began to ache from his uncomfortable position but he hung on grimly, determined to see the end of this midnight journey. But it showed no signs of finishing. They were clear of the outskirts of London now and running through more rural surroundings. The car gathered speed, and he found it increasingly difficult to retain a hold; once, as they bumped over a particularly bad rut, he was almost jerked from his precarious position.

Through a sleeping town he recognised as Luton they sped, out into the open country, again through villages and more towns, thundering over bridges and roaring between the high walls of cuttings. They came through Leicester without slackening speed, and for the first time White began to have an inkling of their destination — Manchester. They were making for the big Midlands city!

He suppressed a groan. Already he was a mass of bruises and aches; by the time they reached their destination, he felt that he wouldn't have a whole bone left in his body. The car slowed a little to negotiate the streets of the town, increasing its speed when it once more reached the country.

There was a grey light in the sky, and a drizzle of rain had begun to fall as they passed through Stockport. If Manchester was their objective, the journey was nearly at an end; and Arnold, stiff, cold and sore, breathed a prayer of thankfulness.

But he was congratulating himself prematurely. Without warning, the car turned off the main road and began to negotiate a series of secondary feeders which got worse and worse until they became little more than cart tracks. Leafless hedges and gaunt trees rose vague and menacing against the grey sky. Arnold was already wet through, and so numb with cold that he could scarcely retain his hold. Would this nightmare ride never come to an end? They came out of a narrow lane, down which the car had bumped violently, swung to the right, and ran along a twisting country road, bleak and inhospitable-looking in the drab grey of early morning. At the intersection of another road he caught a glimpse of a signpost, and managed to decipher the first four letters of the faded inscription — GARS. His imagination filled in the rest: Garston.

So that was where they were going — to the old house where Gloria Swayne had been driven on the night four years ago when she had signed the extraordinary contract drawn up by the mysterious Nottingham Deane. The discovery sent the frozen blood flowing through Arnold's veins quickly. It looked as if he were on the verge of learning something important.

The car slowed and turned in between the crumbling stone pillars which guarded the entrance to a weed-grown and neglected drive, and he took the opportunity to slide from his uncomfortable perch to the ground, falling among a tangle of bramble. There was no doubt that they had reached their destination, and he had no wish to be discovered by the man driving the car. As he picked himself up, he saw it disappear round a bend, and prepared to follow. He was so stiff from maintaining one position for such a long time that he found it difficult to walk at first, but presently, as the circulation restored itself, this passed.

He went forward cautiously, keeping in the shadow of the thick laurels and evergreens that lined the approach. The drive turned abruptly, and he caught his first glimpse of the house — a gaunt, desolate structure surrounded by trees whose interlaced branches almost shut it from sight. In the half-light that preceded the coming day, it looked cold and uninviting. Blinds obscured the windows, lending it a sightless appearance that gave it something of the look of a dead thing. Before the pillared portico the car had come to a halt, and he could distinguish the driver vaguely as he stooped into the interior.

The man straightened up, half carrying, half dragging the apparently unconscious figure of Mr. Grandsire. Staggering over to the entrance, he mounted the worn steps, and, depositing his burden in the porch, fumbled in the pocket of his heavy coat for a key. Watching, Arnold saw that he had some difficulty in opening the door, but he managed it at last, and disappeared into the house, carrying the limp form of the old man. The door shut, he heard the slam of it, and then there was silence, silence and no sight of life or movement except the motionless car.

He began to move nearer up the drive. It broadened into what had once been a gravel crescent, but was now so over-grown by grass and weed that it looked like an unkempt lawn. Into this near the house branched a secondary path, a narrow tunnel that ran under a broken-down pergola that obviously led round to the back of the premises. Arnold decided to explore.

He picked his way cautiously over great trailing branches of rambler roses that had fallen from their supports and lay tangled across the path. As he had expected, it led round by the side of the house to the rear. He passed by a large greenhouse the glass of which was broken in a dozen places, and came to a big neglected garden lined by close-growing trees. The grass of the lawn was waist high, and what had once been flower beds were a mass of dead sticks and lush growth. A forlorn sundial, like a forgotten gravestone, protruded from the waste of grass and weeds. The general atmosphere was infinitely depressing, more so in the drizzle of rain and the eerie greyish light that preceded the dawn.

Halting under cover of a clump of rhododendrons, Arnold considered the situation. His greatest desire was to discover the identity of the man who had driven the car, and next to this was a wish to prevent any harm coming to the old man who had been forcibly brought to this desolate and neglected place. In order to achieve both these objects, it was necessary for him to gain admittance to the house — a risky proceeding, since the man who had come there would be on the lookout. Still, however risky it was, it was necessary, and he decided that the greenhouse offered the best means of doing so.

Cautiously he emerged from his place of concealment, crossed the narrow path, and paused by the crazy glass structure. One of the panes was missing near where he stood, and he concluded that it would not be difficult to squeeze through the aperture it had left. Thrusting in his head, he listened, but he could hear nothing. A shelf ran round three sides of the place, supporting a collection of cracked and empty flowerpots and a few that contained the withered remains of flowers. A dead grapevine grew up in one corner, its twisted branches spread pathetically across the sloping roof. A pair of French windows that evidently gave admittance to one of the lower rooms occupied the centre of the fourth wall. Faded yellow blinds were drawn down behind the glass, and he could see nothing of what lay beyond. Hoisting himself up, he wriggled with difficulty through the small square aperture and, crawling over the broad shelf beyond, dropped among the litter of rubbish on the concrete floor. Crossing to the closed French windows, he listened once more. No sound came to his ears. The house might have been tenantless except for the fact that he had seen the unknown man enter.

Stretching out his hand, he grasped the handle, and to his surprise and delight he found that the windows were unlatched.

Pulling them open gently, he stepped into a dark and musty-smelling room. It was so dark that he could see nothing, but he guessed that it was furnished from the feel of the carpet beneath his feet. Keeping his hands outstretched before him to warn him of possible obstructions, he advanced carefully. A piece of furniture loomed up in front of him, and he avoided it; and presently, as his eyes grew accustomed to the gloom, he was able to make out a fairly large room, comfortably furnished in a rather old-fashioned way as a breakfast room. Opposite the French windows by which he had entered was a closed door, and to this he made his way. Like the window, it was unlocked, and he peered out into the dark passage.

The dim light, which had percolated through the greenhouse and faintly illumined the room in which he stood, failed to penetrate as far as this, and he could see nothing. Neither, although he listened intently, could he hear anything. He went forward, feeling his way with the utmost care and longing to switch on the torch in his pocket.

He guessed that he had emerged into the passage. By extending his arms, he found that his fingertips touched a wall on either side. Remembering the outside shape of the house, he decided to turn to the left, concluding that this would bring him to the hall. And eventually it did, as he discovered when his hands touched the carved rail of the banisters. There was still nothing but darkness around him, and he paused, irresolute, at the foot of a staircase — the main staircase, he thought, by the feel of the newel post.

What should he do next? He had succeeded in entering the house, but without light or sound to guide him, it was difficult to tell where he could locate the man of whom he was in search. And then, while he was trying to make up his mind about his future actions, he heard a sharp crack from somewhere close at hand above his head. The sound had come from up the staircase, and its suddenness startled him. He heard the swish of air as something whistled downwards, experienced a sudden agonising pain in his head, and knew nothing more.

21

The Telephone Message

Trevor Lowe stood in the big hall at the Providence Mission with Superintendent Jameson. An uneasy and rather scared Mr. Willis had just admitted them.

The dramatist had come post-haste from Portland Place after receiving Jameson's news, picked up the superintendent at the station, and gone round with him to the Prov. The disappearance of Mr. Grandsire worried him. Had the old man got frightened at his questions on the afternoon of the Simmons murder and bolted, or was there a more sinister explanation? He remembered the man whom the proprietor of the mission had referred to as Collins but whom the detective was pretty certain concealed the identity of the bell murderer. Had this man been afraid that Grandsire might be tempted to talk, and spirited him away in order to ensure his silence? It was quite conceivable. If, as Lowe believed, this man was the brother of Sylvia Bell, then naturally Mr. Grandsire would have done his best to shield him. That was evidently the explanation, after the discovery of the murder, of his reluctance to say much concerning the man who had visited him that afternoon.

'Now see here, Willis,' said Superintendent Jameson crossly, 'just you tell us all you know about this man Grandsire, and don't go hiding up anything or you'll find yourself in trouble.'

'I don' know nothin'!' whined Cosh, his usual assertiveness conspicuous by its absence. 'I don' know nothin' about the guv'nor. All I know is that 'e's gone.'

'When did he go?' asked Lowe.

Mr. Willis shook his head. 'I can't tell yer. 'E was there last night when I went to bed and 'e wasn't there this mornin' when I took 'im up 'is tea. 'Is coat and 'at's gone from the 'all, but when 'e went I know no more'n a newborn baby.'

Jameson clicked his teeth impatiently. 'This is going to be a serious matter for me,' he grumbled. 'When I report the fact that this man slipped through my fingers, I'm going to get hauled over the coals!'

''E ain't the only one wot's gone, neither!' said Mr. Willis darkly. 'There was a feller wot come 'ere last night, 'e's gone, too.'

'Oh, who's that?' demanded the superintendent.

'Feller called Charlie Gibbs. I found 'im getting the worst of a scrap outside the Angel. 'E stopped a packet and it didn't do 'is 'ealth no good, so I thought I'd bring 'im along 'ere. 'E 'adn't got nowhere else to go, 'e told me, so I arst 'im if 'e'd like to stop for the night. I fixed it up with the guv'nor, give 'im a meal and he popped off to bed. This mornin', when I goes to the dormitory, 'e's gone.'

'What was he like — ' began Jameson, but Lowe interrupted him.

'You needn't worry about him,' he said. 'I know all about him.'

Mr. Willis turned a surprised face towards him, and Jameson raised his eyebrows. 'Who was he?' he demanded.

'My secretary,' answered Lowe.

Mr. Willis uttered an indignant snort. 'Blimey!' he exclaimed. 'And to think I treated him nice! No wonder 'e was on the side of that blinkin' flatty!'

Jameson looked at the dramatist suspiciously. 'What was your secretary doing here, sir?' he enquired.

'He was here to keep an eye on Grandsire,' answered Lowe, 'and I've no doubt that's the reason why he has disappeared, too. I expect he's following Grandsire.'

'Well, that's something,' said Jameson, a little relieved. 'Maybe we'll get some news through him. Take me up to your employer's rooms,' he said, turning to Mr. Willis.

Cosh hesitated. ''Ere,' he protested, 'you ain't got no right to go pokin' about among his private things!'

The superintendent produced a document and thrust it under Mr. Willis's battered nose. 'Take a look at that!' he snapped. 'And if you've ever seen a search warrant before, you'll recognise it. Now, don't waste any more time!'

Still grumbling but unable to think of a

suitable retort, Mr. Willis led the way up-stairs. The three rooms occupied by Mr. Grandsire were scrupulously clean, and although barely furnished were very neat. There was a small sitting-room, a larger bedroom, and a tiny room that contained odds and ends: a few battered trunks and suitcases and suchlike impedimenta. A hasty search revealed nothing of importance. There were no letters; not a single scrap of paper that was of any value.

They came downstairs again, disappointed, and tried the office, but the door was locked and Mr. Willis affirmed that Grandsire had the key.

'We'll have to break it open then,' grunted the superintendent, but Lowe intervened.

'I shouldn't do that if I were you,' he said in a low voice. 'You've no real evidence to prove anything against Grandsire. There's nothing to prevent a man going away in the middle of the night if he wants to. If you break into his private office, even though you've got a search warrant, and he comes back, he'll be in the position to raise the deuce.'

Jameson saw the force of this argument. None knew better than he the difficulties under which the police had to operate, and even though he was well within his rights in forcing his way into the missing man's private office, he knew that it would go ill with him if Mr. Grandsire liked to complain to headquarters.

'Well, we'll leave it for the time being,' he said grudgingly. 'Now see here, Willis, I'm going back to the station. I want you to notify me as soon as this man Grandsire comes back, or, alternatively, if you hear anything from him.'

'You bet your life I will,' said Mr. Willis.

'Was he in the habit of going off suddenly like this?' asked Lowe.

'No, 'e ain't never done it before. 'E's been away once or twice on business, of course, but 'e ain't never left in the middle of the night without leavin' word. I can't understand it.'

Lowe thought he could understand it, but he had no intention of mentioning the fact. The link between Mr. Grandsire and Nottingham Deane he proposed, for the present, to keep to himself.

'Do you think, sir,' said Jameson, as they went back to the station house, 'that Grandsire was responsible for the killing of that man Simmons?'

'No, I don't. If he was responsible for that murder, then he must have been responsible for all the others.'

Jameson nodded gloomily. 'Why the dickens did he bolt then?'

'We don't know that he has. He may have been called away on urgent business.'

'He wouldn't have sneaked off in the middle of the night!' retorted Jameson. 'He'd have wakened Willis and told him he was going. It looks fishy to me! If he wasn't actually responsible for the murder, he knows a great deal more than he let on.'

Lowe was silent. He was not prepared to deny this, for it was his own opinion.

'I shall get the usual routine enquiries going,' said the superintendent as they reached the station. 'Circulate a description and ask for any information. In the meantime, if your secretary gets in touch, then you might let me know, sir.'

Lowe answered evasively. He had no desire at the present juncture for the police to interfere. The man at the bottom of the bell murders was, as he knew, possessed of abnormal cunning, and the slightest false move would result in his slipping through their fingers. The police were excellent in their way, but they were not noted for their delicacy in handling a situation such as this. Therefore he preferred to use his own discretion whether he should notify Jameson if a message came through from White.

At the back of his mind he felt a little uneasy concerning him, due to the fact that he was not at all sure that Grandsire had disappeared of his own free will. It struck him as unlikely that the old man would draw attention to himself by such a move. There was no reason for him to be afraid, so far as he knew. Although Lowe's enquiries concerning Nottingham Deane had obviously given him a considerable shock, his position was not sufficiently serious to make him run away. Lowe considered that it was far more likely he had got in touch with the man he had called Collins, or that Collins had got in touch with him, and that a meeting had been arranged, a meeting that had probably been witnessed by White. It was this which gave rise to his feeling of vague uneasiness. In a certain sense, the man he was up against was mad, of that he had no doubt, and therefore he would stick at nothing to ensure the successful carrying out of his crazy scheme. It was not so much his own safety that bothered him, or so Lowe read his mind, as the knowledge that any interference at the present juncture would prevent him completing his plan of vengeance. There were still seven men who had served on that jury to be accounted for — unless any of them had died naturally in the meantime — and until they had suffered the fate of the others, the killer would make every effort to retain his freedom.

Obviously Mr. Grandsire, if he knew anything, which just as obviously he did, was a danger; and if White had allowed himself to be discovered following the old man, another danger.

Lowe considered there was every cause for his uneasiness as he made his way back to his flat. However, he could do nothing but await events and hope that his fears were groundless. He had barely settled himself down before the fire in the study when Shadgold arrived.

'Can't stop very long, Mr. Lowe,' greeted the burly inspector, 'but I thought I'd just drop in and give you the result of our enquiries concerning those people on your list.' He took a sheet of paper from his pocket. 'Two of them are dead,' he continued. 'Drinmore died six years ago and Tyler the year before last, so I crossed them off. The others — Hewson, Millward, Cranleigh, Selcourt and Winster — I've succeeded in tracing, and a close watch is being kept on them.'

'Good!' said Lowe. 'That's excellent, Shadgold!'

The inspector nodded. 'I've carried out your suggestions, but I must say I'd like to know something of your reasons for making them.'

'You shall know all in good time. How many of these people live in London?'

'Two. Bryan Millward, the artist — he's got a studio flat in Chelsea; and John Selcourt — he's got a house at Hampstead, a big place standing in its own grounds. Hewson lives at Shepperton, Cranleigh at Gravesend and Winster at St. Albans.'

'Keep them well guarded,' said Lowe seriously, 'particularly Millward and Selcourt.'

'Why those two in particular?'

'Because they live in London, and are therefore more easily accessible so far as our friend the bell-man is concerned.'

'How do you know they're easier to access, Mr. Lowe?' he said sharply. 'Do you mean the killer operates from London?'

'That's my opinion.'

The inspector ran his fingers through his hair. 'Look here, Mr. Lowe, can't you give me a more definite line to this business? Why are these fellows in danger?'

'Be patient for a little while longer,' said Lowe. 'In a few days I hope to be able to tell you everything. In the meantime, take every precaution to see that these five men are closely watched.'

Shadgold protested and argued, and eventually departed in something approaching a bad temper, for Lowe had been adamant.

The dramatist was sipping a cup of tea which his housekeeper had brought him when the telephone rang. Crossing to the instrument, he put the receiver to his ear and was greeted by the nasal voice of the exchange operator.

'Is that Welbeck 78977?'

Lowe agreed that it was.

'Just a moment please,' said the woman, and after a short interval a faint voice came over the wire.

'Hello — Mr. Lowe?' it called.

'Yes. Who's that?'

'White. I'm telephoning from Garston Village, near Manchester.'

The dramatist uttered an exclamation. 'What are you doing there?' he asked.

'I've found the fellow responsible for the bell murders,' answered the far-away voice. 'He's with Grandsire at Garston Manor. Can you come up to the place? I'm keeping an eye on it.'

'I'll come at once.'

'I'll meet you at the entrance to the drive. Are you coming by car or train?'

Lowe considered for a moment. 'I'll come by car,' he said. 'It'll be quicker.'

'I'll explain everything when I see you,' said the faint voice on the wire. 'I'd better get back now. I don't want to be away too long in case they leave.'

There was a click as the receiver was hung up, and Lowe turned away from the instrument with an expression of satisfaction. So White *had* succeeded in following Grandsire when he had left the mission on his midnight excursion. He experienced a feeling of relief as he telephoned the garage for his car. His uneasiness regarding the secretary's safety had been unwarranted.

His relief was premature, as he was to discover before many hours had passed, for Arnold White at that moment was lying bound and helpless and very far away from the call box from which the unknown had sent the message which was to bring Trevor Lowe into the trap that had been prepared for him.

22

Garston Manor

The journey from London was uneventful. The big car ran smoothly, eating up the miles; and as every turn of the wheel brought him ever nearer to his destination, Lowe began to feel a thrill of excitement.

So Grandsire and the unknown murderer were at Garston Manor, the house which belonged to Nottingham Deane and in which Gloria Swayne had, a little over four years ago, signed that contract? The end was in sight. Very shortly now, the killer would be under lock and key, harmless to do further damage.

Lowe slowed and brought the car to a halt at a signpost at a crossroads. An examination showed him that the village of Garston lay four and a half miles ahead, and he continued on his way, the headlights of his car illuminating the gaunt hedges and deserted ribbon of road along which he was travelling.

He came at last to the ancient stone pillars that marked the entrance to Garston Manor, and stopped. He had no wish to advertise his presence, and so before leaving the car he switched off all the lights. The place looked deserted and uninviting; the night was cold, and a chill wind was blowing fitfully so that the skeleton branches of the trees that grew in such profusion in the vicinity of the old house creaked and groaned intermittently.

Although it was not actually raining, there was a damp rawness in the air; and in spite of the heavy coat he was wearing, Lowe shivered as he left the warmth of the car, and, crossing the strip of road, paused to peer up the dark tunnel of the neglected drive.

There was nobody in view, and he hesitated. White had suggested meeting him at this point, but there was no sign of him. Did this mean that the people who had come to this lonely house had left, and that he was following them to their new destination? Or was he somewhere concealed in the tangle of bushes nearer the house and was not yet aware that Lowe had arrived?

He decided to wait for a few minutes. He had run the car close up under the shadow of the straggling hedge that bordered the road, and it was practically invisible. From the house or from the drive, he concluded, it couldn't be seen at all.

He waited for five minutes and nothing happened. There was nothing to indicate a living soul on the place, no sight or sound; only the mournful moan of the wind and the creak of the branches as it swayed the bare trees. He was beginning to think that his first idea was right and that Mr. Grandsire and his companion had left before his arrival, when he heard a faint sound from somewhere in the darkness around him: the soft rustle of bushes.

'Is that you, White?' he whispered.

There was no answer, but the sound was repeated — and then something warned Lowe of danger. But the warning came too late.

Even as he stepped away from the sinister rustling, something crashed with tremendous force on his head. He staggered, flung out his arms, and pitched forward on his face, to lie inert among the tangled weeds of the neglected drive.

His sensation as he came back to consciousness was anything but pleasant. His head was sore and tender, and felt twice its normal size, and there was a restriction to his limbs which had at first puzzled him and then became clear as the full use of his senses returned — he had been securely bound.

He moistened his lips and stared about him. He was in a large room full of dim pieces of furniture that loomed up in the faint light of a single candle which was perched on the corner of a great marble mantelpiece. There was dust everywhere. The thick carpet on which he lay was covered by a film of it, as were the chairs and table. Almost his first conscious thought was a feeling of annoyance at himself for having fallen so easily into the trap which had been prepared for him. He had taken it for granted that the voice

which had spoken to him over the telephone was Arnold White's, although it
had been so faint that he had failed to
recognise it. He had put this down to the
distance and faulty transmission, and apparently he had been wrong. He wondered
with acute uneasiness what had happened
to his secretary, and received an answer
almost before the thought had formed in
his mind, for his roving eyes showed him
that he was not the only occupant of the
room. A few yards from where he lay, he
caught sight of the vague outline of somebody else, and twisting to get a better
view, saw that it was White. He was bound
hand and foot, but unlike Lowe, had had
a gag tied about his mouth.

'Hello!' called the dramatist huskily.
'Are you all right?'

Arnold stirred and turned his head in his
direction, and Lowe saw the movement
with relief. It was something that White
was alive and apparently unhurt. His heart
sank again, however, as he realised the full
seriousness of the situation. He was under
no misapprehension regarding their ultimate fate. The madman into whose hands

they had fallen would never have taken the trouble to lure him to this place unless it was his intention to finish the job properly. He had become aware that Lowe was a danger and would take the only step possible to see that the danger was eliminated.

He tested the cords that bound his wrists, but they were immovable. 'How about you?' he asked, looking towards his secretary. 'Is there any chance of your getting free?'

White shook his head.

'Well, we shall have to make the best of it then,' said Lowe philosophically. 'Is Grandsire here?'

White nodded.

'Where?' asked the dramatist, and he received a negative reply. 'Have you seen anything of the man responsible for getting us in this position?' he continued.

Again Arnold nodded; and then, as his employer opened his mouth to put a further question, a sound at the door stopped him. He rolled over to face it, and as he did so it opened, admitting the figure of a man in a heavy coat, his face concealed behind a handkerchief which had been tied over mouth and nostrils, so that only his eyes were visible. He stood for a moment on the threshold, looking from one to the other. Then he advanced into the room, closing the door behind him.

'Woke up, have you?' he said, speaking in a harsh, obviously disguised voice. 'I thought perhaps you would have done by now.'

Lowe looked at him steadily. 'Even a lunatic has moments of sanity,' he retorted calmly.

The man started, and the eyes above the handkerchief glittered. 'What do you mean?' he asked thickly. 'What do you mean, a lunatic? I'm not mad. I'm as sane as you!'

'You're as mad as a hatter!' said the dramatist contemptuously.

The glittering eyes grew brighter. 'I'm not mad!' he screamed. 'You know I'm not mad! I've been too clever for you, that's all. Too clever for the police! It's a lie to say that I'm mad — '

'It's the truth!' broke in Lowe. 'You're

as mad as your sister was, Sylvia Bell!'

The shot went home. The other staggered as if under a physical blow. 'What do you know about my sister?' he croaked. 'What do you know about her?'

'I know that she killed her husband in a moment of insanity!' snapped Lowe. 'And that her father committed suicide. The taint runs right through the family — Lanter!'

'It doesn't! It doesn't!' cried Lanter, and the dramatist knew that he had touched the one chink in the armour, the one fear that obsessed him beyond all others. 'I'm not mad, I tell you!' He was almost sobbing in his rage. 'I'm not mad! What I've done is justified because my sister was murdered! She was killed for something she couldn't help. She never knew she was responsible for the death of Bell. She wasn't well at the time, and those swine hanged her! Murdered her!' He laughed harshly.

'You'll see whether I'm mad or not. I'll show you! Mad! Could a madman have carried out his plans as well as I have? I've killed five of those twelve men who sent my sister to her death, and I'll kill the other five. I've planned everything, and nobody'll stop me! I was afraid you'd stop me, that's why I lured you here. Mad! Would a madman have thought of destroying that book in which Bookham kept his cuttings for fear the discovery of it might put the police on the right track? Could a madman have covered up his traces as well as I have? Answer me that!'

Lowe was silent. He had no desire to say any more. His taunt had achieved the effect he had wished. In his excitement the man before him had forgotten to retain his disguised voice, and what had previously been but a vague suspicion was now a certainty.

'You've nothing to say, eh?' he went on, and by a supreme effort he had calmed himself. 'Of course you haven't! Every action of mine refutes your abominable suggestion.'

'What have you done with Grandsire?' asked the dramatist.

'He's all right at present. He's here in another room. I didn't want to injure him in any way, but, like a fool, he threatened me. He'd guessed that I'd killed Simmons and he threatened me.'

'You were the man who visited him that afternoon at the mission?' said Lowe, and it was more an assertion than a question.

'Yes, I was the man. Simmons was the next on the list, and I had succeeded in tracing him there. It was a coincidence that he should have gone to Grandsire, to the mission; one of life's little ironies. Grandsire didn't know that he was one of the twelve. While we were casually having tea, I asked him if there was a man called Simmons staying with him, and he admitted that there was, but that he was at that moment in bed in the dormitory because he hadn't been feeling well. That was all I wanted to know. I made an excuse that I wanted a wash, and slipped up to the floor above. I killed him by cutting his throat with a safety razorblade which I found in the bedroom. I'd had no intention of killing him that afternoon — I'd only gone to spy out the land; but the opportunity was too good a one to miss. Two of those men who convicted my poor sister have cheated me — they're dead, but there are still five remaining, five more for me to deal with . . . '

'Don't you think you're very stupid to tell me all this?' said Lowe, and the other laughed.

'If there was the slightest chance of your ever using it against me, I should be!' he retorted. 'But there isn't! Neither you, nor Grandsire, nor he — ' He jerked his head in the direction of Arnold. ' — will ever leave this place alive. Do you realise that?'

Lowe realised it only too well. 'What are you going to do with us? Kill us, as you killed those five unfortunate men and Taverner?'

'Not quite in the same way,' answered Lanter. 'It'll be a long time before anyone discovers you. This house is old, and there is no other habitation within three miles. Well soaked in petrol, it should burn like tinder, and you three will burn with it! Before the fire engines can get here from Manchester, there will be nothing left — nothing but the ruins to act as a gravestone!'

In spite of himself, Lowe shivered. It

was a dreadful finish. His imagination pictured them, bound and helpless, while the old house burned around them. It would be merciful if the smoke and fumes suffocated them before —

'When do you propose to put this diabolical scheme into practice?' he asked, forcing himself to speak calmly.

'Tomorrow night,' was the answer. 'I'm staying here until then, and I'll set fire to the house before I leave. I must be in London between twelve and one; I'm settling accounts with the sixth man who gave the verdict against my sister — John Selcourt. The papers in the morning will be full of another silver bell tragedy, but you won't be alive to read it. Make the most of your time, for you haven't got very long.' He turned, and crossing to the door went out, closing it behind him.

Lowe looked across at White, and in his eyes saw the horror which the madman's words had aroused. 'Cheer up,' he muttered as cheerfully as he could. 'We aren't dead yet.'

He tried to infuse hopefulness into his words, but he saw no possible chance, unless a miracle happened, for any of them. Before the end of tomorrow evening, they would die painfully and horribly, as their captor had planned.

23

Ronald Has an Idea

Ronald Lane sat in Mr. Willis's cubbyhole in the hall at the Providence Mission and stared, with a worried and anxious look, at the battered face of that gentleman.

'But what could have happened to him?' he muttered. 'Where can he have gone to?'

Mr. Willis shrugged his shoulders. 'I don' know nothin' more than I've already told you, Mr. Ronald. You knows as much as I does. The perlice 'as been dodgin' in and out all the blinkin' day, and they don' know nothin', neither. 'E's just gone!'

The young man frowned and bit his lips. He had heard nothing of Mr. Grandsire's strange disappearance until he had dropped into the mission that evening to see his foster-father, and Mr. Willis had broken the news. The information had at first astonished him, then alarmed him. It was the first time such a thing had happened, and it caused him a considerable amount of uneasiness. Except that the man who had adopted him was fairly well-off, Ronald knew very little about his private affairs. There might, quite conceivably, be a very simple explanation for his suddenly absenting himself like this, but it was unlike him to have gone off without leaving some word or message, especially in the middle of the night.

This extraordinary behaviour, coming as it did on top of the murder of Simmons, gave rise to all sorts of wild speculations in Ronald's mind. It was not that he believed for a moment that his foster-father had any connection with that crime; but Mr. Willis, whose ears were phenomenally long and whose hearing was of the keenest, had been able to tell him quite a lot concerning Lowe's visit and the interview he had had with the old man and its culmination. Obviously something had occurred to upset Mr. Grandsire pretty badly, and Ronald, who was as fond of the old man as if he had really been his father, was not unnaturally upset.

'I don't know where he can have gone to,' he said for the twentieth time, shaking his head.

'No more don't I,' declared Mr. Willis. 'No more don't no one. He just hooked it durin' the night and nobody ain't seen 'im since. And that other feller — 'e went with 'im. It's my belief,' he added darkly, 'that the perlice knows more than wot they let on. Maybe they've got the guv'nor 'id up somewhere and is puttin' the third degree on 'im.'

'Nonsense!' said Ronald impatiently. 'That sort of thing doesn't happen in this country!'

'Nothin' the perlice did 'ud ever surprise *me*! A nasty, sneaky lot they are, in my opinion. I remember once, before I was a reformed character, when a sergeant got up in the witness-box and the lies 'e told about me ain't nobody's business! And the judge believed 'im, although it was the clearest case of perjury you'd ever come across!'

Ronald was too anxious to listen to the ex-convict's reminiscences. 'I wish we could get into the office,' he said. 'There might be something there that would tell us where he's gone.'

'Mr. Grandsire's got the key,' said Mr. Willis in an injured voice, a little annoyed that his anecdotes had not been received with more interest, 'and without the key, unless you busts the door open, you can't get in!'

'Won't any of the other keys fit?'

'No; the guv'nor 'ad a special lock put on,' he said, omitting to add that this precaution had been taken by Mr. Grandsire in order that no temptation should be put in the way of his reformed porter. 'Not,' he went on, 'that it's much of a lock. One of them flimsy things wot looks all right but wot a child in arms could open.'

Ronald looked up quickly. 'Does that mean you could open it?'

'As easy as kiss yer 'and,' said Mr. Willis contemptuously.

'Then come and do it!' said Ronald, rising to his feet. 'I'll take the responsibility.'

'You mean you — you wants me to pick it?' said the amazed Mr. Willis.

'I want you to do whatever is necessary to open that door,' snapped Ronald.

A slow grin spread across the battered features of the ex-convict. 'Blimey, it'll be like old times!' he exclaimed cheerfully. ''Alf a tick while I gets a bit of wire.' He disappeared into the back regions of the mission, returning shortly with the things he wanted in his hand. Going over to the locked door of the office, he stooped, inserted a piece of stiff wire into the keyhole, withdrew it, twisted the end skilfully with a pair of pliers which he had brought for the purpose, and re-inserted it. After a moment or two's probing, there was a click and the lock shot back.

'There y'are!' said Mr. Willis proudly. 'There ain't another man in the 'ole of England wot could 'ave done the job neater nor quicker.'

Without commenting on this extravagant and immodest statement, Ronald entered the neat office. The desk was in its usual state of tidiness, and for a second or two he hesitated. Was he justified, after all, in examining his foster-father's private papers? In the circumstances, he came to the conclusion that he was.

Three of the drawers of the desk were unlocked, but they contained nothing of importance, mostly headed paper bearing the address of the mission and one or two bills from local shopkeepers. Mr. Willis's special gift had to be called in requisition again to open the locked drawers, and in one of these Ronald made a discovery. In a large envelope he found the title deeds of a house called Garston Manor, made out to a certain Nottingham Deane. The house was apparently situated on the outskirts of a place called Garston, eleven miles from Manchester, and he frowned at the document, a little puzzled. Who was Nottingham Deane, he wondered, and why were the title deeds of his house in the possession of his foster-father?

There was another paper in the same envelope, and this gave him an even greater surprise. It was a contract, properly drawn up and signed, and the signature was that of Gloria Swayne! He read it through hastily, his amazement increasing:

'*An agreement made this twenty-sixth*

day of November, 1932, between *Miss Gloria Swayne, of 104 Brixton Road, and Nottingham Deane, Esq., of Garston Manor, Garston, Lancashire . . .* '

He read through the extraordinary conditions:

'*Consideration of the sum of fifty thousand pounds . . . on condition that the said Gloria Swayne shall remain unmarried for a period of five years from the date of the signing of this contract.*'

What did it all mean? Was this the reason for Grandsire's agitation when he had mentioned Gloria Swayne? Who the deuce was Nottingham Deane?

'Found anythin'?' Mr. Willis's voice broke in on his thoughts, and he saw the eyes of the little man regarding him seriously.

'Have you ever heard my father speak of a man called Nottingham Deane?' asked Ronald.

Mr. Willis screwed up his face, scratched his head and then shook it. 'No,' he answered. 'I ain't.'

Ronald folded the contract and the title deeds and slipped them into his pocket. He continued the search, but found nothing else of interest. 'Come on,' he said, and he pushed the disappointed Mr. Willis out of the office. 'Can you lock the door again?'

Mr. Willis fumbled with his piece of wire and then straightened up. 'There y'are,' he said. 'No one 'ud know it 'ad ever been opened, not unless they was told.'

'Then you needn't tell anybody!'

'Am I likely to?' said Mr. Willis indignantly. 'Wotcher take me for?'

He waited, hoping that the young man would take him into his confidence regarding the contents of the two documents he had removed from the envelope in Mr. Grandsire's desk, but his hopes were not realised. Lighting a cigarette, Ronald thought rapidly. On the face of it, there seemed nothing in either of the two papers in his pocket that supplied a suggestion for Mr. Grandsire's strange disappearance. And then an idea occurred to him. Perhaps Gloria Swayne could help. She had signed that contract and would know all about it.

The thought had no sooner entered his mind than he acted on it. With a muttered word to the aggrieved Mr. Willis, whose curiosity was at fever heat, he left the mission; and after some difficulty, for they were prolific in Stepney, succeeded in finding a taxi and was driven westwards.

Gloria was in and showed her surprise when he was announced.

'I'm terribly sorry to trouble you, Miss Swayne,' stammered Ronald — it always annoyed him that he felt so shy and embarrassed in this woman's presence — 'but I believe you may be able to help me.'

The surprise in her eyes deepened. 'In what way?' she asked.

He plunged into an account of Mr. Grandsire's disappearance, and produced the documents he had found in the desk. 'This contract is signed by you,' he finished, 'and I thought perhaps . . . perhaps — '

'Let me see it,' she broke in, and stretched out a hand. He gave it to her. 'Yes,' she said gravely. 'I signed this a little over four years ago. You found it in Mr. Grandsire's desk?'

He nodded.

'Extraordinary!' she murmured. 'I think I'd better tell you the whole story, Mr. Lane, and then you'll know as much as I do.'

Almost word for word, she repeated the story she had told Trevor Lowe, and Ronald listened, his astonishment showing plainly in his face.

'Evidently my father knows this man Nottingham Deane,' he said when she had finished.

'He must do,' said Gloria, 'seeing that you found that contract in his desk.'

'Do you think that's where he could have gone? To see Deane?'

'It seems likely,' she said, her face puzzled. 'But where?'

'To Garston Manor,' said Ronald; and then, as a suggestion occurred to him: 'I say, Miss Swayne, supposing — supposing I'm right — that my father has gone to meet Deane. Wouldn't it be a good idea if — if we went along, too?'

'To Garston, do you mean?' she said quickly.

He nodded. 'Yes. If this man Deane is at the manor, it would give you an

270

opportunity to talk about this contract.'

'When are you thinking of going?'

He looked at his watch. 'It's too late tonight, and I've got an appointment in the morning. What about tomorrow, immediately after lunch?'

'I'll be ready.'

'Then I'll get a car and call for you at two o'clock tomorrow.'

He left her full of excitement at the prospect of at last meeting the mysterious Nottingham Deane, and discovering the reason why he had suggested that extraordinary contract — so excited that she scarcely slept all night. Neither did Ronald, though his restlessness was due to a different reason. On the morrow he would have an opportunity of spending several hours in the company of the woman who had scarcely ever left his thoughts from the moment he had first met her.

24

The Last Moment

Darkness merged into light with a slowness that was almost incredible. After that one visit, Lanter had kept away; and although they had heard him moving about in the house, they had seen nothing of him. Neither food nor drink was brought to them, and in consequence they were both hungry and thirsty; they could have dispensed with the food, but the longing for something to moisten their dry lips and parched throats became, as the hours dragged by, almost unbearable.

Again and again they had attempted to free their wrists, but without result. The cord was stiff and the knots had been tied skilfully and tightly. The dramatist had even tried, by rolling over to the secretary, to untie the knots with his teeth, but this also had been futile. He had, however, succeeded in loosening the gag sufficiently for White to shake it free, which was something. Arnold had tried the same thing with the cords at Lowe's wrists, but the knots were in such a position that they were impossible to get at, and the result was no better than the dramatist's had been. The removal of the gag, however, if it did nothing else, enabled them to talk to each other, and this was a relief. They both realised how futile any attempt would be on their part to raise an alarm. The house was isolated, and no one was likely to hear them. All they would do would be to bring their captor post-haste to replace the gag.

The grey of the dawn brightened. Through the chinks in the blinds that covered the windows of the long room, they saw the faint gleam of a pale sun. They had discussed every likely and unlikely plan they could think of to escape the fate their captor had planned for them, but none of them offered even the smallest chance of success.

Throughout the hours of the long night they had lain wakeful, staring into the darkness, for the end of candle on the mantelpiece had quickly burnt itself out; and towards noon Arnold dropped into a fitful doze, a condition for which Lowe was thankful. At least it would ease his mind and temporarily erase the thought of what lay in store. There was one pleasant thought amid the gloomy imaginings which had occupied his mind: the thought that Lanter would at least pay the penalty for this terrible thing he contemplated. For although he was ignorant of the fact, when he attempted to add John Selcourt to his list of victims, he would walk into a trap. He must be completely unaware that Lowe had arranged with Shadgold to have all the remaining members of that jury closely guarded and watched. It was something, at least, to know this, though it would benefit themselves not at all.

The time passed so slowly that they might have been confined for a month in that room instead of only for a few hours. Arnold had just awakened, and the light outside was beginning to fade once more, when without warning the door opened and Lanter came in. He was dressed as he

274

had been before, and he carried in his hands two square tins that were unmistakable. Lowe set his teeth as he recognised them. So the time had come!

Setting them down, the man advanced and stood for a moment, looking at them through the gloom in silence. 'I'm about to leave for the last time,' he said. 'I have certain preparations to make for my — er — interview with Selcourt tonight, which necessitates that I should be in London in good time. Therefore I cannot delay longer in taking my departure.'

'You think you're going to get away with it?' said Lowe. 'You think you can commit this terrible crime and the further crimes you contemplate and escape scot free?'

'Why not?' demanded Lanter. 'I know you think I'm mad, but it isn't the act of an insane man to plan so carefully ahead to eliminate all danger. I shall succeed, and when I've accomplished my purpose, I shall be satisfied. It occurred to me,' he went on, coming closer, 'that before carrying out my little scheme for wiping the three of you off the earth, I should take the precaution to see that there's nothing on you which might later serve as a means of identifying your remains. I've already done this with Grandsire. It struck me early this afternoon that it would be artistic.' He bent down as he finished speaking, and rapidly went through the contents of Lowe's pockets, piling them in a heap on the dusty carpet.

The dramatist's notebook, in which he was in the habit of jotting down such items as were better not left to his memory, interested him. Pausing before transferring his attentions to White, he carried the little book over to the window and rapidly turned the pages. Watching him, Lowe suddenly felt his heart sink. On one of those pages he remembered having written a list of the remaining members of the jury, adding a note to remind him to tell Shadgold to have them guarded. Was the last triumph to be snatched away from him?

He was quick to learn. Lanter suddenly turned from the window and came back. 'So,' he said softly, 'you've taken the precaution to have these enemies of my family watched by the police. It won't save them, but I'm glad to know of it. Had I not found this book, I might have run my head into a noose!'

'You'll do that eventually anyhow!' said Lowe curtly.

'Indeed?' said Lanter, and there was a sneer in his voice. 'It's most refreshing to meet a man as confident as you. Even I, with my superior intelligence, wouldn't like to make such a sweeping assertion.'

He slipped the little book into his pocket, gathered up the rest of the things he had piled in a heap beside Lowe, and stowed them away in another. Going over to White, he stripped the secretary of every movable object he carried and added these to his collection.

'Now,' he said, 'I doubt if anything will be found when the fire has burnt itself out. You may as well have company, though, for your last moments.'

He went out and was gone for some time. When he returned, he carried the bound form of Mr. Grandsire in his arms. Depositing the old man on the floor, he gave a quick glance round, went over to the two tins, and unscrewed their metal caps. One at a time, he picked them up and scattered their contents about the room. The pungent odour of petrol came to Lowe's nostrils.

'I'm using more in this room than any other part of the house,' explained Lanter conversationally, 'because I wish the fire to be concentrated more here than anywhere else. The whole should burn like tinder; it's very old and there's a great deal of timber in its construction. I won't bother to gag any of you; it's completely unnecessary. However loudly you may shout, your voices won't carry beyond the confines of the grounds. Your car I've already disposed of. During the night I drove it into a wood several miles from this place, where it's unlikely to be discovered for some time. When it is, there'll be no hint to show what's happened to its owner. I'm telling you all this to prove how wrong you were in your assertion that my brain's unbalanced. No man whose mind was not under complete control could take into account all these things and deal with them.'

He finished emptying the last tin, and surveyed his handiwork with satisfaction. 'I must go now,' he said. 'I wish you a pleasant passing. In any case you'll be warm enough.' He chuckled at his own joke and went out, this time leaving the door open.

They heard him go through into the back of the house, and Lowe looked across at the figure of the old man lying helpless a few yards away from him. 'Is there any chance,' he whispered, 'of freeing your hands?'

'None!' answered Grandsire hoarsely. 'I've tried again and again. This is my fault. I should have come forward and told the police all I knew, but it's too late now.'

'I'm afraid it is,' said Lowe, and the words had hardly left his lips when a flickering sheet of flame illumined the dusk of the hall.

A door banged, and they heard hurrying footsteps go by the window. The flame died down, then leaped to greater brightness, and the sharp crackling of burning wood mingled with the noise of a starting engine. A billow of blue smoke rolled into the room, laden with the tang of burning oil. It would not be long before the air caught . . .

Lowe clenched his hands until the nails bit into the palms, and the perspiration started out on his forehead. The light beyond the door into the hall grew brighter, a flickering red glow through which shot tongues of yellow, and the crackling increased. A faint murmuring sound like the hum of a million bees grew momentarily stronger . . . A gigantic dancing shadow of the staircase was thrown on the blank wall of the passage opposite . . . The smoke grew denser, and with it came a puff of hot acrid-smelling air that caught them by the throat and set them coughing . . .

With smarting eyes, Lowe watched the illuminated oblong of the open door. How long would it be before the flames reached them? Even as the thought crossed his mind, a curling tendril of yellow licked the frame, flickered, went out, and flickered again . . .

The roar was louder now as the fire

caught hold, and the incessant crackling was like a miniature bombardment.

'I'm afraid it's the finish!' muttered Lowe hoarsely, and Arnold White replied with a nod. He was beyond speech. He felt that if he unclenched his teeth to speak, he'd scream.

'My God!' gasped Grandsire. 'Can nothing be done?'

'Nothing can save us now except a miracle!' croaked the dramatist, and the shy tongue of flame that had been dancing in and out of the doorway became bolder and ran up the woodwork to the ceiling . . .

Another appeared on the other side, blended with the first, vanished, came again, and — stayed. The wood of the doorway was burning!

The hall beyond was lit up by a fierce red glare through which volumes of blackish smoke rolled sluggishly. A blue haze hung above them, obliterating the ceiling and momentarily descending as it was fed from the raging holocaust outside. There was a crash, and a shower of sparks flickered through the red mist, and Lowe guessed that the banisters had fallen . . .

The heat was intense, the air heavy and fume-laden, held little oxygen, and made them breathe more quickly. The flames round the door frame were spreading. In a very little while now, the petrol-soaked carpet would catch . . .

A flicker ran from the door across the bare boards to the edge of it, failed to hold, and went out. A second flicker followed, and the carpet burst into flames. The fire rushed across the material like a flood. The smoke grew thicker, the air more difficult to breathe. The hungry flames reached the curtains at the window, licked at them, and consumed them . . .

The walls were no longer visible. In the centre of the rapidly decreasing oasis of carpet, they lay watching the raging fire coming nearer and nearer . . . The heat was now blistering. Lowe saw the perspiration pouring down Arnold's face and realised that he himself was wringing wet. Breathing became an agony, like swallowing mouthfuls of molten lead . . .

Closer and closer came the ring of fire,

and Lowe felt his senses swim. The floor on which he lay rocked dizzily like a ship in a stormy sea . . .

He heard, as from a great distance, the shattering crash of breaking glass and a husky scream, and with the cry ringing in his ears fell into a seemingly bottomless pit of blackness.

25

A Race Against Time

Cool air blowing across his face brought Lowe back from that abyss of darkness. He opened his aching eyes to the sound of whispering voices, and stared up at the two dim figures that bent over him. From somewhere came a lurid glare, an uneasy flickering light; and in this uncertain radiance he made out with astonishment that one of the people standing near him was Gloria Swayne. There was a man with her whom he did not recognise.

At first he thought he was dreaming. Perhaps this was all an illusion; perhaps he was still unconscious from the heat and fumes of that last dreadful moment in the burning room. And then, as he revived, he knew that there was nothing unreal about these two people.

With a sigh, he struggled up on one elbow, discovering that his hands were free and that he could move his legs easily. At the movement, they turned towards him.

'He's recovering,' said Ronald, and Gloria uttered a little exclamation of relief.

'How — how did you get here?' muttered Lowe in a cracked and husky whisper.

'We'll tell you presently,' Gloria said. 'Don't worry now. Are you all right?'

'Yes. But what about the others? My secretary and the old man?'

'They're all right,' answered Ronald. 'I managed to get you all out in time . . . '

Ronald's face was blackened and his clothes singed, and he looked a wild and unkempt figure as he stood in the half dusk, lit up every now and again by the flames from the burning house. It had been touch and go. He and Gloria had arrived in time to see a column of smoke rising from the doomed building. Their astonishment had been great, and leaving the car, they had run up the drive. They could see the glow of the fire from inside, and guessed that it had taken too great a hold for anything to be done to save the house. While they had watched, uncertain what they should do, Ronald had heard a hoarse cry come from amid the smoke and flames. It was the cry that Lowe had vaguely heard ringing in his ears as he lost consciousness; the cry that Arnold White had involuntarily given as the tight hold which he had kept over his nerves gave way.

Ronald had forced his way through the flames and discovered the three of them, bound and helpless, in the blazing room, and with difficulty, for the place was like a furnace, had succeeded in smashing open the French windows and dragging them to safety. His hands were burned and blistered and his clothes were alight in a dozen places before he had accomplished the rescue. White was the only one who was still conscious. The old man and Lowe were senseless, and Mr. Grandsire had not yet come round.

'How did the place catch on fire?' asked Ronald. 'It couldn't have been an accident. I smelt petrol — '

'It wasn't an accident,' croaked Lowe

hoarsely. 'It was deliberate, a deliberate attempt to put an end to us!' He sat up and stretched out a hand. 'Help me up,' he said. 'I think I'll be all right.'

Ronald gripped the hand and pulled him to his feet. For a moment or two he swayed dizzily, leaning on the other's shoulder; and then, as the cool air soothed his tortured lungs and cleared his head, the faintness passed. 'I'm all right now,' he muttered. 'What about the others?'

'I'm all right,' called Arnold in a cracked voice; and looking round, Lowe saw that he was sitting up, rubbing his left arm from which the coat sleeve hung in shreds. 'What I wouldn't give for a glass of water is nobody's business.'

'I could do with a drink myself,' admitted his employer.

Accompanied by Ronald and Gloria, he walked unsteadily over to where Mr. Grandsire lay, a prone, motionless figure.

'I don't think there's anything serious the matter with him,' said Ronald. 'His heart's beating fairly strongly and he's breathing well.'

Lowe stooped with difficulty and

looked at the old man. His face was blackened with smoke and his eyes were closed.

'I think he'll be all right in a moment,' he said, and as he spoke there was a dull crash behind him, and a shower of sparks went scurrying into the darkening sky. 'There goes one of the floors,' he muttered.

'Oughtn't we to get in touch with a fire brigade?' said Gloria.

Lowe pursed his lips. 'The nearest must be miles away. I don't think it's much good. By the time they get here, the place will be nothing more than a heap of smoking ruins.'

'Who — who was responsible?' she asked.

'The same man who was responsible for killing Taverner and those other unfortunate people. The bell murderer!' He looked at Ronald. 'I don't think I've met you before, but I'm infernally grateful for what you've done, both you and Miss Swayne.'

'My name's Lane — Ronald Lane,' answered the young man.

A light of understanding came into the dramatist's bloodshot eyes. 'Then you're Grandsire's adopted son?' he said, and

Ronald nodded. 'I think we'd better get him away from here as soon as possible,' he went on. 'How can we manage it?'

'I've got a car at the end of the drive,' said Ronald. 'We left it there when we saw the smoke and came the rest of the way on foot.'

'That's excellent!' said the dramatist. 'I think I'm strong enough to help you carry him.' Except for an intense thirst and the pain from one or two slight burns, he was feeling fairly fit, considering the terrible ordeal from which he had just emerged. Between them, they succeeded in lifting the senseless figure of the old man and carrying him down the weed-grown drive, followed by Gloria and Arnold. The car Ronald had hired was a speedy-looking coupe, and into the seat next the driver they succeeded in propping Mr. Grand-sire.

'I don't know how we're all going to get in,' said Ronald, eyeing the machine doubtfully. 'The dickey-seat 'ull hold wo.' He pulled it open as he spoke.

'Mr. White and I can sit there,' said Gloria, 'and there'll be room for you and

Mr. Lowe in the front.'

Ronald helped her in and Arnold followed. It was a tight squeeze for the three of them in front, but they managed it, and the young man took the wheel.

'There's a village a few miles away,' he said. 'We passed it on the way from London. I think that's the best place to make for.'

Lowe nodded. 'Stop at the first inn,' he said, and as the car moved forward: 'Now tell me how you managed to get here so opportunely.'

Ronald told him, and Lowe listened without comment.

'I don't know what it all means,' concluded Ronald, 'or who this man Nottingham Deane is, but it was providential that I found those documents in the desk.'

'It was,' agreed Lowe heartily. 'And as far as the identity of Nottingham Deane is concerned, I think I can enlighten you. Nottingham Deane is a name used by your foster-father for purposes of his own.'

'I guessed it might be something like that,' muttered Ronald. 'But why?'

'It's too long a story to tell you now. But he had a very good reason, I can assure you.'

'It's — it was — it was nothing that could get him into any trouble? He hasn't done anything — ' He left the sentence unfinished, but Lowe knew what he was driving at.

'No, no!' he said reassuringly. 'You needn't worry about that.'

An expression of relief crossed the young man's face. 'It did worry me a little,' he admitted. And nothing more was said until they reached the village and drew up outside the entrance to a small public house.

It was not yet opening time, and they had to knock for admittance. The landlord, a red-faced countryman, listened to their story with round eyes.

'You'd better bring the gentleman into the bar-parlour,' he said, and Mr. Grandsire was carried in and laid on a horsehair sofa. 'Doctor Handley's house is a few doors up the road. Perhaps you'd like him to come along?'

'Yes, send for him, will you?' said Lowe,

and taking the brandy which Ronald had secured, he forced a few drops between the old man's lips.

They heard the landlord calling to someone, and presently he returned to inform them that his son had gone on the errand. During the interval, Lowe consumed a large tankard of beer, and never had anything tasted so delicious.

'That's better!' he said as he set down the empty mug. 'My throat was like a rasp.'

'And mine,' put in White, who had joined him. 'All I want now is a couple of pounds of steak and some fried potatoes, and I'd feel fit for anything.'

'I'm afraid you'll have to postpone that,' said his employer. 'We've got work to do, and none too much time to do it in.' He glanced at the clock over the bar. 'It's just six, and we've got to be in London before that crazy devil carries out his threat on Selcourt.'

'What do you mean?' asked Ronald; but before Lowe could reply, the landlord came in accompanied by a small dark-featured man whom he introduced as Handley.

Lowe made a quick examination of the unconscious man and looked up. 'He's had a very severe shock,' he said. 'It's nothing very serious, but he mustn't be moved. He needs complete rest.'

They looked at each other, and Ronald turned to the landlord. 'Have you got a room you could let us have?' he asked.

The man nodded. 'Yes, sir, I can let you have a bedroom.'

'Then get it ready,' said Ronald, 'and we'll get him to bed at once. You go back to London with Mr. Lowe,' he added, turning to Gloria, 'and I'll stop here and look after my father.'

She hesitated.

'Yes, that'll be the best thing,' broke in the dramatist before she could reply. 'You can come back with us, Miss Swayne, and we'll drop you at your flat.' He took Ronald by the arm and led him to one side. 'We must go now,' he said. 'It's urgent that we should reach London before twelve.'

It was ten minutes past six when they left after a hasty wash, and at the first town they came to, Lowe filled up with petrol and put a call through to Scotland

Yard. To his annoyance, Shadgold was out, and he found he had wasted several precious minutes for nothing. Although John Selcourt was being watched, the fact that Lanter had become aware of this worried him. The man was cunning, and quite capable of eluding the vigilance of the watcher.

They made good time until they reached Derby, and here disaster overtook them. The engine began to misfire, coughed, spluttered, and finally stopped, refusing obstinately to restart despite all their frantic efforts to make it. Fortunately, the breakdown had occurred near the town. Had it been in the open country, it would have been fatal. As it was, more precious time was wasted while they went in search of a garage and hired another car.

It was just striking ten when they reached Leicester, two thirds of their journey completed. They were both ravenous, and Lowe stopped at a public house and bought sandwiches, putting through another call to the Yard. Shadgold was still out. The official in charge thought he had gone off duty for the day.

He came back to the car a little irritable and annoyed, and they continued on their way, munching the sandwiches as they sped along.

Mile after mile reeled by. Lowe's smarting eyes peered steadily at the road ahead, although his lids were heavy with sleep and he was half dead with weariness. Arnold White had fallen into a doze, and he did not wake until, covered with dust and with the radiator cap steaming, Lowe brought the car to a halt outside the block of flats in which Gloria lived.

'Get out quickly, Miss Swayne,' said the dramatist. 'I'm sorry to hurry you, but I can't waste time.'

She nodded. 'Good night, Mr. Lowe. I'll see you tomorrow.'

The car moved off before she had crossed the strip of pavement, for they had still to get to Hampstead, and the hands of the last clock they had passed had pointed to a quarter to twelve. Lowe had considered stopping and ringing up Hampstead police station, but there was no time for this. By the time he had explained and the orders had been issued, it might be too late.

At the end of Frognal, he pulled the car up and enquired his way from a traffic policeman. The man gave him his directions, and as they set off, a clock somewhere near at hand boomed twelve. He set his teeth. They had cut it fine, but they might be in time!

The car negotiated a series of side turnings and came out into a broad thoroughfare that ran by the edge of the heath. Turning the car into a side street, Lowe stopped it and got out.

'We'd best leave it here,' he said. 'If we leave it near the house, our man will spot it and be warned. Come on.'

Without waiting to see whether White was following or not, he hurried up the road. The house he was in search of proved to be at the other end, a big grey-stone building surrounded by a high wall, behind which rose a screen of trees. Halfway along its length, the wall was broken by a wide arch in which were set two iron gates. Lowe tried them. They were locked.

'We'll have to climb over,' he said, and

springing up, he caught the coping of the wall with his hands and a second later was astride. Reaching down, he helped Arnold to follow, and they dropped into the shrubbery on the other side.

Pushing their way through this, they came out onto a gravel path and saw the house before them. It was in complete darkness, and there was not a sound anywhere. Lowe frowned. He had kept a sharp lookout for the Yard man who should have been on guard, but he had seen no sign of him. Unless he was keeping watch from inside, which seemed very unlikely, he had either been withdrawn, or something had occurred to take him away from his post.

The dramatist was uneasy as he began to make a tour of inspection round the house. The path they were on encircled it, and as they reached the back of the premises, he suddenly gripped White's arm and pointed to a window on the ground floor which was half open.

'Look!' he whispered. 'He's here!'

26

Danger by Night

He climbed in cautiously through the open window and waited for White to join him. When they were both standing in the semi-darkness, they looked round and discovered that they were in a small cloakroom, the open door of which gave on to a long passage.

'He'll be upstairs,' whispered Lowe, his lips close to his secretary's ear. 'We'd better make our way through the hall.'

They came out into the passage, and proceeding along it presently arrived at the foot of a wide flight of stairs which disappeared into the darkness above. Lowe paused to listen before ascending, but no sound reached his ears from the sleeping household. He wondered for a moment whether he had made a mistake regarding that open window. There was just a chance that it might have been overlooked by the servants before they retired for the night.

Stealthily they crept up the big staircase and arrived on a broad landing. Again the dramatist stopped, listening, but still no sound reached him. On either side of the landing stretched a gloomy corridor. Suddenly he saw something which caused him to press White's arm warningly.

'Look,' he breathed.

With narrowed eyes, Arnold peered into the shadows of the right-hand corridor. For a moment he could see nothing, and then he made out a tiny pin-point of light that gleamed like a glow-worm ahead. It was moving erratically away from them.

'Somebody's moving along there,' whispered Lowe tensely, and he knew in that instant that the open window had not been the result of carelessness, but that the man they were after had arrived to carry out his threat.

Softly they advanced along the corridor, following the dancing light until it suddenly disappeared. Lowe stopped.

'He's gone into one of the bedrooms,'

he said in such a low tone that the words were scarcely audible. 'We've got to hurry!'

Moving swiftly forward, he reached the spot where the light had vanished. There were two doors here next to one another, and he looked at them for a second indecisively.

'Which one?' he muttered.

The question was dramatically answered. From the room immediately opposite where he stood came a smothered scream.

Without a second's hesitation, he burst open the door and entered, feeling for the switch as he did so. By a lucky chance, his finger connected with it at once, and as he pressed it down, the room became flooded with light.

The man who was standing over the bed sprang back with a snarled oath, the long knife in his hand glittering in the light. Beyond, Lowe caught a momentary vision of an elderly man raised up on one elbow, his face distorted into an expression of horror that in any other circumstances would have been ludicrous.

He had little time for more than a fleeting vision, for with amazing swiftness

Lanter recovered from his astonishment and sprang at him.

Lowe warded off a downward thrust from the knife he held and it flew from the man's hand. Before he could get a grip on him, however, he hooked the dramatist's feet from under him. He lost his balance, crashed heavily against a table, and overturning it fell with it to the floor.

The killer sprang for the doorway and collided with Arnold White. The violence of the impact knocked them both breathless for a moment. The noise had wakened the house, doors were opening, and voices were calling in alarm. Lanter staggered back against the doorframe, but recovering himself, darted out into the passage. As he reached the top of the staircase, a light was switched on from below, and with a stifled oath he turned to retrace his steps.

Arnold, still a little dazed from the collision, tried to tackle him as he came charging back, but Lanter lashed out and caught him a glancing blow on the side of the head. White retaliated by shooting out his foot, and the other stumbled over it and went sprawling. He was up again in a second and continuing his mad race down the corridor. In the meanwhile, Lowe had managed to scramble to his feet and appeared at the open door of the bedroom.

'Where is he?' he gasped.

Arnold pointed a finger towards the flying figure, too breathless for speech.

Lowe set off in pursuit, but the other had gained a good start. There was a window at the end of the passage, and the dramatist heard the sash flung up with a squeak. For an instant, he glimpsed the man he was after scrambling over the sill, and then he disappeared from sight. He tore up to the open window and leaned out. The man was scrambling quickly down the thick ivy that covered the back of the house, and without hesitation Lowe swung his legs over the sill and began to follow. Ten feet from the ground, Lanter dropped and flew across the lawn, disappearing into a dense patch of shrubbery. The snapping of breaking branches and the rustling of leaves came to Lowe clearly as he landed lightly on the gravel path, and he sped off in the direction taken by his quarry. He reached the bushes and forced his way through, but there was no sign of Lanter.

He came to a wall, the continuation of that which ran level with the street; and as he did so, he heard the whine of a car. It receded in the distance, and realising that further pursuit was useless, he retraced his steps to the house.

The front door was open, a stream of light flooding out into the darkness. In the centre of this, standing on the top step, was the dishevelled figure of a small rotund man dressed in dressing gown and pyjamas, his hair awry, peering fearfully out into the night.

'What's been happening?' he gasped. 'Who are you?'

'Get on the telephone to the police!' snapped Lowe. 'Tell them to come round here at once!'

He pushed past the frightened man and entered the hall. At the top of the staircase, he met Arnold.

'Did he get away?' gasped the lad.

His employer nodded. 'Yes. It doesn't matter very much, though. At least we were in time to prevent him from carrying out his threat.'

There was an interruption from the passageway behind them. The bald-headed man, whom Lowe had seen for a moment in bed, was coming unsteadily towards them, his face wearing an expression of surprised indignation.

'What is the meaning of all this?' he spluttered angrily. 'Who was that man in my room? What the devil are you doing here?'

'If I hadn't come here, Mr. Selcourt,' answered Lowe grimly, 'you would have been dead by now, and the newspapers would have carried another account of a silver bell murder tomorrow!'

'What?' gasped Selcourt, his face turning white. 'What do you mean? How do you know this? Who are you?'

Briefly the dramatist explained the situation, and there were beads of perspiration on the stout man's face when he had finished.

'You astound me!' he muttered huskily.

'I'm sorry I was so abrupt, Mr. Lowe, but naturally I had no idea ... I'm most infernally grateful. *Wilkins!*' He leaned over the banisters and shouted to the dishevelled little man below. 'Bring some whisky to my study at once.'

'Yes, sir,' quavered Wilkins. 'What was it, sir? Burglars?'

'Don't ask questions!' snapped Selcourt. 'Do as I tell you!'

'And then ring up the police!' put in Lowe.

He followed Selcourt down the stairs to a cosy room leading off the hall, and the scared Wilkins swiftly arrived with a tray of drinks. Lowe gulped down the whisky that Selcourt mixed for him, and felt better. He heard the muffled voice of the servant speaking from somewhere, and presently the man appeared in the doorway and announced that the police were sending up immediately.

'You'll be able to explain to them, Mr. Selcourt,' said Lowe. 'I haven't time to wait. I must go after this man who broke in here tonight.'

'I shouldn't think there was much

chance of finding him now,' said Selcourt as he helped himself to a second drink. 'He's had plenty of time to get clear away.'

'You needn't worry about that,' said the dramatist quietly. 'I know exactly where to find him, and before the morning I don't think he'll be in a position to do any further harm.'

27

Shadgold Dreams

Detective-Inspector Shadgold left Scotland Yard early, after a tiring and unproductive day, to seek the solace and comfort of his small house at Kennington. Not, he thought gloomily, that there would be much comfort, for his wife was away on a visit to relations, which meant that he had to shift for himself.

However, it was a relief to get away, if only for a little while, from his cheerless office and the worries and cares that beset him.

The bell murders were getting him down. It was becoming increasingly difficult to satisfy the impatience of an irate assistant-commissioner. It had worked very well at first when he had reported that he was following up an important clue and expected developments at any moment; but when nothing materialised, something more concrete than this vague assertion was demanded of him, and he could not supply the demand. It was all very well, he thought irritably as a bus carried him homewards, for Trevor Lowe to suggest that he should do this and do that, but it didn't go far to satisfy the practical mind of the commissioner. Why couldn't he be a little more explicit? If he knew anything, why couldn't he say what he knew? This passion for keeping everybody in the dark until he had the whole thing cut and dried was very unsatisfactory.

Acting on his suggestion, Shadgold had arranged to have the people he had mentioned watched, but it had not been by any means an easy matter. When he had asked for the men necessary for this job, his immediate superior had, not unnaturally, wanted to know why these people were in danger from the Bell man, and he had been quite unable to tell him. He had to make the excuse that he was merely working on a supposition, and wished the matter attended to purely as a precautionary measure.

Superintendent Miller had grumbled. They were short-handed. To provide the necessary men, it would mean taking them off other duties; and unless Shadgold could provide a more concrete reason, he didn't consider that he was justified in doing this.

The inspector, who had great faith in his friend in spite of his predilection for keeping things so much to himself, argued and protested and eventually got what he wanted, although the permission was given grudgingly and reluctantly.

It was not surprising, therefore, that he was not in the best of tempers as he inserted the key in his front door and entered his small abode. The fact that there was no meal prepared for him, or anybody to get it ready except himself, did nothing to minimise his irritability. He cooked himself a steak, boiled some potatoes, and supplementing this meal with a bottle of beer, satisfied his hunger. When he had finished and cleared the dishes away, he felt better, and settling himself in a chair, lit a cigar and thought over the situation.

There was no doubt that Lowe had something up his sleeve. Past experience had proved over and over again that he was only mysterious when he was on the point of bringing a case to a successful conclusion. When he was completely at sea, he was willing enough to discuss the matter from all angles; but once he had grasped the thread that he thought would lead him to the ultimate solution, he became as silent as a dumb man.

Shadgold derived some consolation from this fact. Lowe, at the moment, was being very mysterious indeed, and therefore should be very near to discovering the truth concerning the series of crimes which had baffled the police. One thing was certain, thought the inspector: something would have to occur during the next two or three days or he was going to find things very unpleasant indeed. The assistant-commissioner had already hinted that unless results could be achieved, he would be taken off the case, which would mean a mark against his name; and up to now his record was unblemished.

He went to bed, his mind still occupied with fruitless conjectures, and for a long time lay staring into the darkness of his room, physically tired but too mentally active to sleep. Eventually he dropped off into an uneasy doze, a slumber that was disturbed by disjointed dreams and visions . . .

He found himself stumbling through a long barren valley paved with huge stones. There were thousands of these of all sizes and shapes, dazzling in the blazing sun that streamed relentlessly down. Suddenly the assistant-commissioner appeared.

'You must leave no stone unturned, Shadgold,' he chanted in a singsong voice. 'No stone unturned.' He pointed along the boulder-strewn way. 'Go on! Look under every stone. You must leave no stone unturned. You must find the bell. Leave no stone unturned!'

Shadgold began to struggle with the huge boulders, the assistant-commissioner dancing along beside him. One after another he lifted and turned over, his arms aching, the perspiration pouring down his face. But there was nothing underneath.

'Go on!' sang the commissioner, when he paused for breath. 'Go on! Leave no stone unturned!'

311

'Don't be silly,' said a voice. 'He'll never do it that way.' And miraculously the commissioner vanished and Trevor Lowe appeared in his place. 'I'll show you were the Bell is,' said the dramatist. 'Lift *that* stone.'

He pointed to a massive lump of rock, and with a tremendous effort Shadgold succeeded in turning it over. Bedded in the mud beneath was a small silver bell. As he looked he saw another, and another. There were hundreds of them, thousands, welling up from a hole in the ground which the stone had concealed.

He was standing knee deep in the little bells and they shifted uneasily, like quicksilver. The whole valley became filled with a tinkling which grew louder and louder as the number of the bells increased, until the noise was deafening.

He tried to close his ears and — awoke with a start, the shrill sound of the bells still ringing in his head.

He sat up quickly, staring, heavy-eyed, into the darkness. The ringing was very real, and as the mists of sleep dissolved from his brain, he realised that it *was* real.

312

The telephone bell in the hall was shrilling a summons . . .

Blinking himself fully awake, he swung out of bed and fumbled with his feet for his slippers. Crossing the room, he opened the door and went stumbling down the stairs. The ringing had stopped, but as he approached the instrument it began again. Lifting the receiver, he put it to his ears.

'Hello!' he called, his voice husky with sleep. 'Who's there?'

'That you, Shadgold?' came the clear voice of Trevor Lowe over the wire.

'Yes,' grunted the inspector. 'What is it?'

'Can you meet me outside the Pavilion, in Piccadilly Circus, in half an hour?'

'What's the idea, Mr. Lowe?'

'I thought you'd like to be in at the death, that's all. I want you to come and arrest this man responsible for the bell murders!'

'You want me to — what?' gasped the inspector, wondering if he was still dreaming.

'To arrest the bell murderer,' repeated Lowe. 'Don't forget — the Pavilion, Piccadilly Circus, in half an hour!'

There was a click as he rang off, and Shadgold, dazed and bewildered, staggered back to his bedroom. For a minute or two he sat on the edge of the bed, rubbing his eyes, and then, springing to his feet, began to dress feverishly.

A call to the nearest rank brought a taxi to his door, and with a curt order to the driver he sprang in and was driven to the meeting place. Lowe was waiting when he got there, although it was well under the time stipulated.

'What's all this, Mr. Lowe?' grunted Shadgold. 'Are you serious? Have you really found this fellow?'

'Am I likely to have rung you up at this hour for a joke?' said the dramatist. 'Yes, I've found him.'

'Who is he?'

'A gentleman called Lanter. He doesn't live very far from here, and we're going round to take him now.'

'But — ' began Shadgold.

'Don't talk — listen! I've got a lot to tell you.'

Rapidly, Lowe related all that had happened since he had last seen his friend, while the inspector, his eyes bulging and his mouth open, listened amazed.

'Good Lord!' he exclaimed when Lowe paused. 'But you don't expect him to go back to his flat?'

'I do,' said the dramatist. 'I don't think he has any idea that I'm aware of his real identity.'

Shadgold mopped his face. 'I suppose there's no doubt?' he said. 'It's going to be awkward for me if there's any mistake, Mr. Lowe.'

'You needn't worry. There's no mistake.'

'We oughtn't to waste any further time then, in case he gets the wind up and tries to make a getaway.'

'White's watching the flat now in case anything like that should happen. If you're ready, we'll go.'

Lowe set off along Piccadilly towards Hyde Park Corner with Shadgold at his side, and the inspector was so astonished at the revelation that had been made to him that he kept silent until they reached the big building in which the man responsible for the bell murders lived.

28

The Bell Murderer

Lanter dropped from the top of the wall surrounding Mr. John Selcourt's house to the pavement, staggered for a moment, recovered his balance, and ran swiftly up the road to the side turning where he had left his car.

He was breathing heavily as he climbed into the driving seat and fumbled with his foot for the starter. The engine hummed rhythmically, and pressing on the clutch, he let in his gears and sent the machine moving swiftly forward. Tearing off the handkerchief he had used to conceal his face, he threw it on the empty seat beside him and turned the car westward. He was shaking with rage, and his distorted face above the wheel was the face of a devil.

Everything had gone so smoothly until that instant when he had swung round from the bedside of his intended victim to face, in the sudden glare of light, the last man he had expected to see. The watcher had been disposed of without difficulty. Warned by what he had read in Lowe's little notebook, Lanter had been on the lookout for the guard the police had stationed to see that no harm came to Selcourt. The man had been strolling leisurely up and down opposite the main entrance to the house, and Lanter, walking boldly up to him, had enquired the way to a mythical address. The rest had been easy. A swift blow with a small rubber cosh he had brought for the purpose, and the watcher was no longer a source of danger. He made doubly sure with a strong dose of chloroform, and disposed of the unconscious man in the garden of a nearby house. By what miracle had Lowe succeeded in getting away from Garston Manor? How had he managed to escape from the fire? It was immaterial really. The only fact of importance was that he had escaped, and had arrived at the house in Hampstead in time to frustrate his plans.

Lanter's lips curled back from his teeth

with a snarl. His ungovernable temper, which had more than once brought him into trouble, threatened to break loose beyond control. It was only by a supreme effort that he mastered his rage. It was necessary that he should think coolly calmly. The fact that Lowe had escaped had increased his danger, although he considered there was no immediate cause for alarm. At the same time, he would have to move warily. He wasn't quite certain how much the dramatist knew That he knew a great deal was certain but did he know the one vital thing Lanter was under the impression that he did not, but was it worth risking this supposition? If Lowe did not know that important fact, then there was no need to worry at all. He could postpone his plans for a week or two, a month or two i necessary, and resume them when a more favourable opportunity presented itself for he had no intention of giving up finally his scheme of vengeance against the men who had brought in that verdic at his sister's trial.

He slowed the car at the entrance to a

garage, turned it skilfully into the sloping concrete runway, and brought it to a halt near a number of others that were ranged in orderly rows under the big glass roof. An attendant came forward, and leaving it in his charge, Lanter muttered a 'good night' and made his way towards the block of flats in which he lived.

An automatic lift took him to the fourth floor, and he let himself into the spacious flat. The married couple who looked after him were away. He made a point of sending them away whenever he had one of these delicate little operations to attend to, wisely considering that it was best that his movements should be known only to himself.

Removing his hat and coat and hanging them tidily in the lobby, he passed into the comfortably furnished sitting-room and poured himself out a stiff whisky and soda. His rage had abated. They never lasted very long, those swift storms of fury that overtook him. The main question that occupied his mind was his safety.

Lowe knew him as Lanter, but did he know him in his other capacity? Would it be more sensible to make a run for it while he had the chance? He dropped into a chair, and lighting a cigarette considered his problem carefully, a second drink at his elbow. If Lowe was not aware of his second identity, then it would be the most foolish thing in the world to flee, for it would be as good as a signed confession. He did not see how Lowe could possess knowledge, for there was nothing to connect Eric Lanter, the brother of Sylvia Bell, with this other personality. He had been at pains to ensure that the two identities were kept separate. It had been essential to his purpose. Neither could any proof be found to link him with Lanter, except — yes!

He went cold as he remembered something that had slipped his memory — Grandsire. Grandsire knew. Grandsire knew him in both his capacities. Had Grandsire escaped that holocaust at Garston Manor? If Lowe had, it seemed only natural that the others had, too.

He got up and began to stride rapidly up and down the room, his brows drawn together, his eyes narrowed to slits. What should he do? There seemed only one thing for it: to get away before the police came knocking at his door.

He felt the hot flush which heralded one of his attacks of rage begin to creep over him, and fought it back. He must keep cool! He must allow nothing to interfere with the ice-cold working of his brain, for this was a tight corner. It never occurred to him that he could not find a solution. The supreme egotism which was the greater part of his nature assured him that he could never be caught. It was only a question of a little thought. What a fool he had been not to make more certain that Lowe and the other two could not testify against him. Why had he placed all his reliance on the fire doing its work when a bullet would have been so much surer? And yet the fire had seemed certain enough. Who could have foreseen that those three people could have escaped the flames? Even now it seemed incredible. How on earth had they managed to get away from that doomed house . . . ?

He pulled himself up sharply. It was

useless allowing his mind to dwell on that. It was merely a waste of time. His own immediate future was of far greater importance.

He forced himself to concentrate, but he was unable to think of a solution. The danger was imminent. If Grandsire had opened his mouth, then he might expect Lowe and the police at any moment . . .

A cold sweat of fear broke out on his forehead. Before his eyes rose the picture of a crowded court, the judge, the jury box . . . the jury who had sent his twin sister to her death! Anything but that!

He ground his teeth. Mad! That was what Lowe had said. That was what the doctor in California had said. Perhaps that was what they'd try and do, lock him up, keep him confined for the rest of his life in a small room with padded walls as they had done before . . . They should never do it! He'd show them how clever he was even yet . . .

The veins in his temples swelled and a mist began to float before his eyes. He steadied himself. What was he *doing*, allowing his mind to drift into these side channels when it was so necessary that he should concentrate . . . concentrate . . . concentrate . . .

How funny Sinclair had looked when the knife entered his chest. He remembered the surprised expression on his face and laughed. The laugh sounded loud in the quietness of the room and startled him. What had made him think of Sinclair? What had Sinclair got to do with the problem of safety? To Hell with Sinclair . . .

Simmons had been sleeping when he had drawn the razor blade across his throat. What a funny little choking gurgle he had given as he died . . .

He passed a shaking hand across his wet forehead. Why couldn't he keep his mind on the matter in hand? Why *would* it keep trailing off? He must get away. There was no question about it, he must get away . . .

Mad! That was what they thought him. Lowe had taunted him with it. Mad! He'd prove to them, once and for all, whether he was mad or not . . .

Get away. Yes, that was what he must

do, get away . . . But where? Where could he go? At any moment now, they might be knocking at the door. If he left the flat, he would find them waiting in the darkness at the head of the lift shaft. Probably they were there now, laughing at him, whispering among themselves that he was too crazy to take advantage of the chance offered him . . .

What chance was offered him? He ran his fingers through his thick hair. Why *couldn't* he think clearly? He was tired, that was it. He needed a rest. A short sleep would clear his brain.

He went over to the door and stopped abruptly with his hand on the handle. What was he dreaming about? There was no time to *sleep*, no time for anything. At any moment now, they might be coming for him to drag him through the dark streets and lock him in a cold cell . . .

Perhaps Bookham would keep a copy of the account of the trial as he had kept those cuttings of his sister's ordeal . . . There he was now, coming out into his little shop to see who the customer was who had called just before closing time. There he was, with blood on his grey hair ... It wasn't Bookham, of course it wasn't Bookham; it was Reiss who hung there swaying before him. Bookham was dead. He remembered killing him and pinning the little bell on his coat. But Reiss was dead, too. Who, then, was this, this little fat man with the bald head and the wound in his forehead ... ?

He stared down at the expanse of dove-grey carpet that covered the sitting-room floor. There was no one there. Neither Bookham nor Reiss nor Stone! How could any of them be there? They were dead, all dead ... He must concentrate. The time was slipping by, and he was no nearer to deciding what he was going to do. Why did these dead men keep coming into his thoughts to destroy his chance of safety?

Was that why? Were they hounding him to the grave to which he had sent them ... ? There was Simmons now, grinning and mouthing at him ... And Sinclair pointing an accusing finger, and Stone, and Reiss and Bookham crowding in the doorway . . .

The blood pounded in his head. He faced those grinning phantoms and spoke to them. 'Go away!' he said between his teeth. 'Go away! You're dead men — dead men! Go back to the place from which you've come!'

But they remained, crowding closer, jostling him and whispering triumphantly as he cowered back . . .

A sudden rage took possession of him and he struck out wildly right and left. They were there to prevent his escape. Lowe had sent them. Lowe, who had died in the blazing house at Garston. Lowe, who had taunted him with being mad . . .

He had expected the police, and these had come instead — these dead men, who jibbered and grinned and laughed at him . . .

'Go away!' he shrieked. 'Go away, I tell you! You're dead, all of you. I killed you. I killed you, I tell you!'

But they pressed closer around him stretching out hands to grasp him . . .

He fought them off, his fury increasing as his wild blows took no effect. His face was flushed with the violence of his exertions, and the veins stood out thick and blue on his temples. Something inside his head snapped suddenly. He clawed the air frantically, staggered backwards, and collapsed across the arm of a chair . . .

And so Lowe found him when he came in the early hours of that morning with Shadgold to arrest him for the crimes he had committed, and the dead man's face was so distorted and his expression so dreadful that it was a long time before the inspector could bring himself to believe that it was really Julian Shuberg at whom he looked!

29

The Verdict

Trevor Lowe had a private interview with Jonathan Grandsire on the evening of the day following Julian Shuberg's death, and much that transpired between them was never made public. The old man had completely recovered from the shock brought on by his terrible experience at Garston Manor, and listened gravely to the news which the dramatist brought.

'Of course,' finished Lowe, 'you knew it was Shuberg?'

'I guessed,' said Mr. Grandsire sorrowfully. 'How did he die?'

'The police doctor said it was a clot of blood on the brain. In a way, I'm glad. It's going to save a lot of trouble.'

'For Gloria?'

'Yes,' Lowe replied. 'The whole story would have had to come out, and the papers would have eagerly seized on the relationship.'

'But surely,' Mr. Grandsire's voice held an astonished note, 'it will come out anyhow?'

Lowe looked at him steadily. 'Why should it?' he asked. 'No one, with the exception of you and I, know that Gloria Swayne is Ann Bell, your granddaughter. She's unaware of it. She's unaware who her parents were. Is there any reason why she should be enlightened?'

The old man looked doubtful.

'You realise,' went on Lowe, 'the shock it will be to her if she should ever learn the truth. She'll go through life with a constant and ever-present dread that the taint of madness may be in *her* blood. Would you willingly inflict such a terrible burden as that on anyone?'

The old man's face was troubled, and he hesitated before replying.

'But supposing this — this taint *does* exist?' he said slowly. 'What then, Mr. Lowe? Supposing Gloria Swayne marries, and that twenty-four year old tragedy is repeated?'

'If I can assure you on the highest authority that no trace of the homicidal

329

mania which was present in her mother exists in Miss Swayne, will you then be disposed to keep silent?'

Mr. Grandsire nodded. 'Yes! Most certainly,' he answered eagerly. 'Believe me, Mr. Lowe, I have no wish to inflict such a terrible scourge on anybody. At the time, I hated the child of my son's marriage. It was only natural, for I loved my son, and his death was a great shock to me. I couldn't bear even to look upon the child. And that's how I lost sight of her. Then gradually I came to see that it was unfair that the sins of the parents should be visited on the children. From that moment, I was determined to find her and do my best, which brought into existence Nottingham Deane. My fear that there should be a repetition of that dreadful crime at Norwood prompted me to include the five-years marriage clause. I concluded that by that time the taint, if it was there, would have shown itself. I did that then because I didn't want to spoil Gloria's life by telling her the truth. How are you going to prove that she hasn't inherited this dreadful thing?'

'I've already been in touch with Sir Robert Taylor, Anthony Hasland and Sir Gilbert Hyde,' said the dramatist. 'They are, as you probably know, the three greatest alienists in the country. I suggest that Miss Swayne is invited to dinner to meet them. Of course, she won't be informed of the reason or who they are. They'll adopt fictitious names for the occasion. It's quite possible, without other examination, for specialists such as these men to pronounce a verdict. Are you agreeable?'

'I'm only too pleased,' declared the old man heartily. 'And if the verdict is favourable, you can count on me, Mr. Lowe, to keep her parentage a secret.'

'Thank you,' said Lowe. 'I believe you will be doing a fine thing, Mr. Grandsire. And now, there's one point which I think you can clear up. Why did Lanter, or Shuberg, postpone his scheme of vengeance for so many years?'

'For quite a simple reason,' said the old man. 'He was in California earning a precarious living which I obtained for him at one of the film studios when the news of his twin sister's death reached him. The shock was so great that he went mad. For twenty years he was confined in a mental home. It was only four years ago that he was released as cured.'

'I see,' said Lowe, and he nodded thoughtfully. 'They were twins, eh? That accounts for a great deal. There's a greater bond between twins than between ordinary children. You knew, of course, at the beginning, that Lanter was responsible for these bell murders?'

'I guessed. The little token and the names of the people convinced me. But until recently, I had no idea that Shuberg and Lanter were one and the same. I wasn't definitely sure until that afternoon when he came to see me at the mission, and I recognised him . . . ' He moistened his lips and his eyes clouded at the recollection. 'When on my return I discovered what had happened, I knew who was responsible.'

'You should have spoken then.'

'I realise that, but you can understand my position. I had no desire to revive interest in the tragedy of my son's death. I was foolish — perhaps criminally foolish.'

The dramatist said nothing. By keeping silent, the old man had been the means of bringing about a further tragedy.

'The moment I heard of the first bell murder,' went on Grandsire, 'and suspected Lanter, I engaged a man whom I knew — his reputation is not of the best, and I think he's pretty well known to the police — to make enquiries. I reasoned that moving as he did among the underworld, he'd be able to hear something. But he was able to tell me nothing. He could neither trace nor had he heard of anyone by the name of Lanter. Of course then I did not know he'd changed his name to Shuberg.'

'I suppose he did that when he was released from the mental home,' said Lowe.

'Yes, I suppose so. No doubt he wished the name of Lanter to be forgotten. Had people connected him with the man who had been shut up for so long, he would have found work difficult to obtain. He was a brilliant director.' He shook his head sadly. 'A genius. I've seen some of his pictures . . .'

'There's a very thin line,' remarked Trevor Lowe, 'between genius and madness.'

*　*　*

The party of seven who sat down to dinner in a private room at the Ritz-Carlton was a gay one. Gloria Swayne, looking lovely as usual, was in her brightest mood. The cares and troubles of the past weeks had gone, and the three distinguished-looking men who, with Trevor Lowe, Ronald and Mr. Grandsire, made up the remainder of the party, listened to her lighthearted chatter with approval. And if they watched her with an attention that was not entirely compatible with good manners, she was unconscious of it.

When the meal was over, Lowe and Mr. Grandsire, making some trivial excuse to Ronald and Gloria, took the other three aside.

'Well?' said the dramatist softly.

'Not a trace,' grunted Sir Gilbert Hyde. 'You agree with me?' He looked at his companions.

'Absolutely!' declared Anthony Haslan. 'The woman's as sane as I am.'

'I entirely concur,' said Sir Robert Taylor.

'There's no doubt of that?' insisted Lowe. 'You could tell — '

'You could tell immediately,' answered Hyde. 'It would be visible in hundreds of small ways.'

The dramatist breathed a sigh of relief. 'You're satisfied?' he asked, looking at Grandsire.

'Completely!' said the old man. And his eyes, which had grown very soft, were looking towards a corner of the big lounge where Ronald and Gloria were sitting together . . .

Books by Gerald Verner
in the Linford Mystery Library:

THE LAST WARNING
DENE OF THE SECRET SERVICE
THE NURSERY RHYME MURDERS
TERROR TOWER
THE CLEVERNESS OF MR. BUDD
THE SEVEN LAMPS
THEY WALK IN DARKNESS
THE HEEL OF ACHILLES
DEAD SECRET
MR. BUDD STEPS IN
THE RETURN OF MR. BUDD
MR. BUDD AGAIN
QUEER FACE
THE CRIMSON RAMBLERS
GHOST HOUSE
THE ANGEL
DEATH SET IN DIAMONDS
THE CLUE OF THE GREEN CANDLE
THE 'Q' SQUAD
MR. BUDD INVESTIGATES
THE RIVER HOUSE MYSTERY
NOOSE FOR A LADY